MY MOTHER'S HOUSE
and
SIDO

Colette

MY MOTHER'S HOUSE
and
SIDO

Translated from the French
by Una Vicenzo Troubridge and Enid McLeod
Introduction by Judith Thurman

Farrar, Straus and Giroux
New York

Farrar, Straus and Giroux
19 Union Square West, New York 10003

Copyright © 1953, renewed 1981 by Farrar, Straus and Giroux, LLC
Introduction copyright © 2001 by Judith Thurman
Printed in the United States of America
My Mother's House originally published in 1922 by Ferenczi, France,
as *La Maison de Claudine*
Sido originally published in 1930 by Ferenczi, France
Published in 1953 in the United States by Farrar, Straus and Young
(now Farrar, Straus and Giroux, LLC)
Second Farrar, Straus and Giroux paperback edition, 2002

Library of Congress Cataloging-in-Publication Data
Colette, 1873–1954.
    [Maison de Claudine English]
    My mother's house ; and Sido / Colette ; translated from the
French by Una Vicenzo Troubridge and Enid McLeod ; introduction by Judith Thurman.
        p. cm.
    ISBN 0-374-52833-0 (pbk. : alk. paper)
    1. Colette, 1873–1954—translations into English. 2. Colette,
1873–1954—Family. 3. Colette, Gabrielle Sidonie, 1835–1912.
4. Authors, French—20th century—Biography. 5. Colette family.
6. Mothers—France—Biography. I. Troubridge, Una Vicenzo.
II. McLeod, Enid. III. Colette, 1873–1954. Sido. IV. Title.
V. Title: My mother's house ; and Sido. VI. Title: Sido.
PQ2605.O28Z466913 2002
843'.912—dc21

2001054460

www.fsgbooks.com

1   3   5   7   9   10   8   6   4   2

CONTENTS

Sidonie-Gabrielle Colette was born in the Burgundian village of Saint-Sauveur-en-Puisaye on January 28, 1873, and died in Paris, on her fur-covered divan in the Palais-Royal, on August 3, 1954. She was given a state funeral—the first for a *citoyenne* of the Republic—and mourned as a national treasure.

Death's protocols, however, had always repelled her and aroused her instincts for impiety. Colette was a pagan whose life and appetites were Olympian in their vitality, as was her oeuvre. She published nearly eighty volumes of fiction, memoir, drama, essays, criticism, and reportage, among them perhaps a dozen masterpieces. *Gigi*—written in the bleakest months of World War II—is the best known to English-speaking readers, somewhat unfortunately, if only because its promise of happiness so misrepresents Colette's view of love.

Like Proserpina, she has two guises: one as a daughter, one as a queen. The daughter of Ceres is our guide to the earthly paradise: the quintessential countrywoman, poet of nature, epicure, coquette, traveler, animal lover, gardener, athlete, collector of butterflies, and connoisseur of sensual pleasures. The realm of the queen is an erotic underworld where love is perdition, where those who give pleasure can't receive it, or those who take it can't give it, and "restless ghosts" crash "headlong and sidelong against that barrier reef, mysterious and incomprehensible, the human body" (*The Pure and the Impure*).

Literary masters as diverse in temperament as Marcel Proust and François Mauriac knew Colette well and considered her great. Her influence is ubiquitous in Simone de Beauvoir's *The Second Sex*. Henry de Montherlant condescended to call Colette France's greatest "natural" writer, though the modifier is something of a slight, not to say a misapprehension—for she was a consummate, even lapidary, stylist who slaved over her sentences and revised prodigiously.

But for the last quarter of a century, Colette has been out of fashion and, in translation, often out of print—or, to borrow an image from *La Naissance du jour* (*Break of Day*), which is probably her most innovative and profound novel—"hiding, like Poe's [purloined] letter, in plain sight." What accounts for her eclipse, particularly during a period when scholars and readers have been so avid to rescue even minor women writers from oblivion?

Colette has always been admirable for reasons that have nothing to do with political correctness. "Me, a feminist?" she scoffed in a 1910 interview. "I'll tell you what the suffragettes deserve: the whip and the harem." She saw no contradiction between supporting conservative positions and living her life as an "erotic militant" in revolt against them. Better worlds and just rewards were of no more consequence to her than the prospect of an afterlife. Preferring "passion to goodness," she seduced her teenage stepson and neglected her only child.

The paradoxes of great literature are those of human nature, and Colette is nothing if not human. "She eagerly picked the fruits of the earth without discriminating those which were forbidden," wrote her stepson as an old man. Accessible and elusive; greedy and austere; coura-

geous and timid; subversive and complacent; scorchingly
honest and sublimely mendacious; an inspired consoler
and an existential pessimist—these are the qualities of the
artist and the woman. It is time to rediscover them.

The provincial backwater where Colette spent her
childhood was known as "the poor Burgundy," to distinguish it from the rich Burgundy of the great vineyards.
Both her parents were outsiders, even pariahs, in the village where they had settled. Her father, Captain Jules Colette, was an officer of the Zouaves from Toulon who,
after his service in the wars of the Second Empire, had
retired to Saint-Sauveur with a wooden leg and a sinecure
as the local tax collector. He proceeded to dabble in sci-
ence, poetry, education, finance, and politics, but failed at
everything he attempted, including paternity—his children considered him a sibling rival. After his death, they
discovered he had spent his retirement tinkering with a
"phantom opus": the luxuriously hand-bound volumes in
his study were, beyond their title pages, entirely blank.
Mme Colette—the splendid earth mother known to
Colette's readers as Sido—was born into a family of
mixed African and Creole descent. Colette would describe
her maternal antecedents as "cocoa-harvesters from the
colonies" (Martinique) and her grandfather as a "ginger-
colored gorilla." But Sido had been educated by her elder
brothers, distinguished liberal journalists who had emi-
grated from France to Belgium. Her wit, atheism, extravagance, and modernity had outraged the villagers nearly
as much as the love affair she had conducted with Captain Colette while she was still married to her alcoholic
first husband. This gentleman died opportunely, leaving
her a fortune that the captain squandered on his improvident dreams.
The "Madame Bovary" of Saint-Sauveur had bound-

less ambitions for her youngest daughter and "second self," Gabrielle, and these never included domestic—or sentimental—drudgery. Sido called marriage, only half-ironically, a "heinous crime," and would rejoice in Colette's liaison from 1905 to 1911 with a cultivated and melancholy lesbian transvestite, the Marquise de Morny, largely because "Missy's" generosity and solicitude were so wholesome for Colette's fiction. Nor was Sido's "precious jewel," childless until forty, ever encouraged by her mother to procreate.

"Balzac has invented everything," Colette wrote in *L'Etoile vesper* (*The Evening Star*), and the writer whom she called "my cradle" and "my forest" could easily have invented the Colettes. The family's dramas in Saint-Sauveur—adulteries, lawsuits, bankruptcies, and suicide attempts—would enthrall its inbred and petty-minded society. However much, in later life, Colette would rhapsodize about her sense of place, and define herself in *Les Vrilles de la vigne* (*Tendrils of the Vine*) as a woman who belonged "to a natal village I have left behind," her voice and character were shaped by her conviction of being "a special case" and her feeling of superiority of the village and its inhabitants.

The young Gabrielle Colette was a rugged, radiant tomboy with sea-green eyes and an auburn plait longer than she was tall. In 1893, at twenty, after a long engagement stalked by scandal, she married Henry Gauthier-Villars, a well-born Parisian rake and journalist of thirty-six who signed his salacious novels and amusingly savage music criticism "Willy." It was a not very well kept secret that all of these extravagantly publicized works had been "improved" by other hands, if not entirely ghostwritten by struggling young writers or provincial academics. It was less well known that Willy had also put his "child bride" to work—and, indeed, Colette would become the most productive draft horse in his stable.

As a nubile literary debutante toiling anonymously for her pudgy *érotomane* of a husband, who not only signed her bestselling Claudine novels[1] and pocketed the royalties but kept her enthralled in more primal ways, Colette invented the century's first teenage girl: rebellious, secretive, erotically reckless and disturbed, determined to be an individual in her own right, but confused about how, or if, one can actually become both a person and a woman. That is a challenge she would take on in her fiction for the next fifty years.

The last fin de siècle was an anarchic and fertile period that generated the anxieties about meaning, authority, and the integrity of the self that we still live with. It was also, not coincidentally, an era of nearly bulimic sexual consumption and pervasive misogyny. Male writers from the most reactionary to the most avant-garde were haunted by the specter of a "virilized," "vampiric" New Woman who, by asserting her rights not only to autonomy but to pleasure, was responsible for the degeneracy of the culture. Women, in turn, were haunted by the consequences of this male fear. Colette, for one, would always struggle valiantly to impersonate a "real" woman (as defined by the old men of her youth), while feeling, as she puts it, like a "mental hermaphrodite."

Writing was the way that a supremely vital and gifted but fragile young woman with a weakness for bondage

1. These are *Claudine at School, Claudine in Paris, Claudine Married, Claudine and Annie,* and *Retreat from Love* (*La Retraite sentimentale*), published between 1900 and 1907, which, as a series, are one of the greatest French bestsellers of all time, if not the greatest.

discovered her true value and disengaged from an ex-
ploitive master. It was not, however, the only bridge to
liberation. Colette had perceived, precociously, that the
beauty of a woman's muscles is identical with their purpose, which is self-support. By 1902, she had installed a
private gymnasium with a trapeze and parallel bars in the
studio upstairs from the luxurious conjugal apartment on
the rue de Courcelles that Willy had financed with her
earnings. And here she began training for the profession
she would take up after their divorce.

"Colette Willy," as she signed the first book Willy gave
her leave to avow—*Dialogues de bêtes* (1904)—also enter-
tained her own small circle of intimates in this "bachelor
pad." Most of them were young, stylish, and "acid-
tongued" gay men—the "valiant of voluptuousness," as
Cavafy would call them. Colette admired their erotic ruth-
lessness and shared their sense of marginality. They con-
firmed her sense—articulated with such eloquence in the
Claudines—that gender is impure; that children of either
sex have drives to dominate and yearnings to be possessed;
that a society which demands too much conformity in the
realm of desire irrevocably warps its young.

In 1905, the year her marriage foundered and she went
off, very publicly, with Missy, Colette also abandoned the
salons of polite society (which closed their doors to her)
and embarked on a stage career. She became a tough,
self-promoting music-hall star—a mime, dancer, and ac-
tress—who was never averse to a skimpy costume or a
kitschy production. It was an interlude for which the
mandarins would never quite forgive her, and every time
in later life her name was proposed for some official
honor, a chorus of elders—recalling how she had bared
her flesh to the leering throng in the two-franc seats and
haggled expertly over her contracts—protested.

Colette's experience of a trouper's life inspired *La Vagabonde* (*The Vagabond*; 1910), a novel that anticipates, by ninety years, the contemporary fashion for wry, first-person narratives by single, thirty-something career women. Its heroine examines her addictions to men with amused detachment, and flirts, alternately, with abstinence and temptation. Is there love without complete submission and loss of identity? Is freedom really worth the loneliness that pays for it? These are Colette's abiding questions.

Her own life as a vagabond and divorcée had exposed her to poverty as she had never known it, and Colette was one of the first middle-class women of her generation to know what it takes—how much passionate steeliness—to earn a living. The frugality of Virginia Woolf's five hundred a year and a room of one's own had as much allure for her as the ideals of Woolf's feminism, which is to say, none at all. Colette's models were never the gentlewomen of letters living on their allowances but the courtesans and artistes she had frequented in her youth, whose notion of a bottom line was fifty thousand a year and a villa of one's own—with a big garden, a great chef, and a pretty boy. They also came closest to fulfilling the ideal of the Amazons: to live unfettered yet sexually fulfilled.

Yet Colette, who entitled her sequel to *The Vagabond*, *L'Entrave* (*The Shackle*), always found it difficult to live unfettered. She had lovers of all ages and both sexes, but as her friend Natalie Barney was to put it in "The Colette I Have Known," "Torn between the desires of her two contrary natures, to have a master and not to have one, she always opted for the first solution." The day she turned forty, Colette was four months pregnant and still performing. By now she had abandoned the selfless Missy to marry her baby's father, Baron Henry de Jouvenel, one of the most influential and sexually charismatic political journalists in Paris.

The child, born in July of 1913, was a daughter to whom Colette gave her own name and her own nickname but not much else, abandoning her to the care of a dour English nanny. She wrote fondly, at times ecstatically, about Colette II, as she sometimes called her, but they only ever shared a roof for the odd month in summer, and the little girl was sent to boarding school at eight, then farmed out to various women friends who acted as Colette's surrogates. "The danger which threatens the writer, elevated to a happy and tender parent, [is that] of becoming a mediocre author," she asserted in *The Evening Star*. There was only one way that Bel-Gazou could make herself exist for her mother, and that was to become her greatest disappointment.

Jouvenel was then the editor of a major Paris daily, *Le Matin*, and in 1911 Colette joined the paper as a columnist, eventually becoming its drama critic and literary editor. Had she never written a word of fiction, she would still be remembered as one of the most original French journalists of the century. Her focus was intimate, but her range was wide. She would be one of the first women to report from the front lines of World War I—having traveled incognito to Verdun in the autumn of 1914 to join her husband, who was fighting with the French army. One of her specialties would be crime, particularly domestic violence and criminal psychology. She wrote about fashion with a knowledgeable irreverence that still sounds provocative today. She penned advice columns on love, food, exercise, decorating, and other traditional woman's-page subjects, but she was lucid and often scathing about the plight of women in brutal marriages and degrading jobs.

In 1916, while on assignment for *Le Matin* in Rome—
the center of the nascent European film industry—Colette also became one of the first twentieth-century
novelists to adapt her work for the new medium. During
the same period, she composed her incandescent libretto
for Ravel's opera *L'enfant et les sortilèges*. But love and war
distracted her from serious fiction. It was not until 1919
that she began to contemplate the story of a beautiful
bad boy living with a courtesan old enough to be his
mother. "For the first time in my life," Colette told a
friend when she had just begun to serialize *Chéri*, "I felt
morally certain of having written a novel for which I
need neither blush nor doubt."

Not all the critics would agree, some calling her in-
comparable portrait of the Belle Epoque demimonde
"soulless," "vulgar," and "perverse." The prevailing opinion, however, was summed up concisely by André Gide
in a now famous fan letter: "What a wonderful subject
you have taken up," he told Colette. "And with what
intelligence, mastery, and understanding of the least-
admitted secrets of the flesh."

After his distinguished wartime service both as a sol-
dier and a diplomat, Henry de Jouvenel decided to enter
politics and ran—successfully—for the Senate. Colette's
erotic legend now became an embarrassment, though not
quite so great an embarrassment as the affair that she had
been conducting with Henry's son by his first marriage.
Bertrand de Jouvenel was a bookish virgin of sixteen
when his stepmother "made him a man" at her beach
house among the dunes of Brittany. She was still smol-
dering and Venusian at forty-seven, even if she did weigh
nearly one hundred and eighty pounds. Her husband,
himself a rapacious womanizer, had tormented Colette

with his infidelities while complaining (not unjustly) of her "monstrous innocence." When he finally discovered her five-year-long liaison with his son and asked for a divorce, Colette was depressed and outraged, but sought solace, as she generally did, by eating "methodically"— her lust for food, she told a friend, "directed primarily at shellfish."

The affair with her stepson and his concurrent romance with a schoolmate his own age inspired *Le Blé en herbe* (*The Ripening Seed*), one of Colette's most sensuously written novels. In comparing the first sexual experiences of a teenage boy and girl, Colette rejects the received wisdom about what the "loss" of their virginity means to men and women. It is the boy who feels most deeply violated and transformed by his initiation. Here, as throughout her oeuvre, the male of the species is the weaker but nobler creature, while the female monopolizes the "will to survive."

Bertrand, who, like his father, had never much liked the "*louche milieu*" of Colette's fiction, wanted her to write something more uplifting. (How exquisitely French: a pimply schoolboy who was honing his sexual technique on the body of his father's wife objected to the absence of any moral feeling in her writing!) In part to appease him, Colette wrote a chaste and celebratory memoir of Sido and her own provincial childhood—*La Maison de Claudine* (*My Mother's House*)—which has become one of the best-loved works in her canon.

Jouvenel and his first wife eventually contrived to separate their son from Colette. She continued to live tumultuously and to write tirelessly, as well as to lecture, travel, edit, and perform. In 1925, during the rehearsals of *Chéri*—she had dramatized the novel and was playing the heroine, Léa—mutual friends introduced her to a worldly

Jewish bachelor of Dutch descent named Maurice Goudeket. He wrote poetry and sold pearls, and he had worshipped Colette's writing since his adolescence. She, in
turn, breathed oxygen into his depressive character and
stifled existence. They embarked upon a torrid adventure
that would in time become the serene and enduring mutual devotion she had yearned for but never known.

The great writer was fifty-two when she fell in love
with the thirty-five-year-old Maurice. After their first idyll
in a rented villa on the Côte d'Azur, Colette bought a
house in Saint-Tropez and settled into the happiest and
most fecund period of her life. This "vintage time" produced *Break of Day, Sido* (a sequel to *My Mother's House*),
La Fin de Chéri (*The Last of Chéri*—a bleak and ambitious
portrait of the lost generation), and a first draft of *Le Pur
et l'impur* (*The Pure and the Impure*—originally called *Ces
Plaisirs . . .*), the work Colette herself judged most worthy
of enduring. It is not only, as she puts it, "my personal
contribution to the sum total of our knowledge of the
senses," but her definitive treatise on the bonds of love—
and on the voracity that bondage seeks to contain.

When the Depression started, Goudeket's jewelry ven-
ture failed, and the lovers—who would marry in 1935 and
honeymoon in New York—decided to embark on a joint
"second career." Rich friends staked them to an *institut de
beauté* on the rue Miromesnil, where Colette did celebrity
makeovers in a white lab coat. They also launched a line
of beauty products: "Colette" potions and cosmetics. The
elegant little boxes bore her signature and her likeness. "I
find the women beautiful as they emerge from beneath
my writer's fingers," she wrote, "and I enjoy touching the
living flesh . . . inspired by a kind of benevolent, maternal feeling." But Colette's genius was not maternal, and
less benevolent than one might suppose. Perhaps that's

why the beauty shop was a failure: the aging actresses who entrusted her with their faces emerged from their makeovers looking twice as old as when they had gone in.

After this strenuous, costly, and disappointing experiment, Colette resumed her primary vocation with renewed vigor. In 1935, she was elected to L'Académie Royale de Langue et de Littérature Françaises de Belge, and the same year her peers voted her the greatest living master of French prose. That virtuosity is nowhere more evident than in *Mes apprentissages* (*My Apprenticeships*; 1936), the most confessional of her memoirs, sober in its power, cold in its passion, in which she takes exquisite revenge on Willy for having destituted her of the Claudines. What sweeter recompense for the frauds perpetrated by a hack than to make him the villain of a masterpiece?

Given her lifelong indifference to politics, it is not surprising that Colette's work of the 1930s ignores the rise of fascism, the general strikes, the unemployment crisis. Her trio of Depression novels—*La Chatte* (*The Cat*), *Duo*, and *Le Toutounier*—are variations on one of her constant themes: the tragic incompatibility of men and women. Yet the superb short stories collected in *Bella-Vista* (1937) manifest a social conscience that is rare if not unique outside her journalism, and their achievement has been compared with the "social portraiture" of Gorky.

The novella, as Goudeket would put it in his memoir, *Près de Colette* (*Close to Colette*), "was henceforth her preferred genre. It represented neither an impoverishment nor a loss of patience, but a willed divestment." And he is right: readers searching for Colette at her purest will find her in the late novellas. It is as if she were adjusting her style, like a diet, to a more sedentary and less flamboyant life.

By the outbreak of the Second World War, Colette was suffering from the excruciating arthritis of the hip—an ailment common among so many dancers—that would eventually cripple her entirely. In 1940, she and Goudeket briefly sought refuge from the German invasion with her daughter, who owned a ruined castle in the Corrèze and was active in the Resistance. Without any means of support, however, they returned to the capital, where they had recently moved to an apartment at 9, rue de Beaujolais, on the *étage noble* of the Palais-Royal—Colette's last and most famous Parisian address. For a while, they both naïvely believed her eminence would protect Maurice from persecution by the Nazis, and for the next four years Colette would practice what she liked to call *"le sage repliement sur soi"*—the wise retreat into one's private bastion—which also translates, less poetically, as lying low.

Colette's work, and even her letters from the Occupation, contain no outrage, and indeed very little apparent cognizance of the war's obscenity. The Paris she observed from her windows overlooking Richelieu's gardens was peopled by a race of beasts and humans with her own virtues of old-fashioned stoicism and female resourcefulness. And like so many of her peers, she contributed her fiction and her journalism to the organs of the pro-Vichy and pro-Nazi press.

Never are Colette's "powers of denial," as she put it, greater than in her short fiction of the 1940s: *Gigi*, *Le Képi*, *Le Tendron* (*The Tender Shoot*), *L'Enfant malade* (*The Sick Child*)—and never is she more endearing or accessible. Perhaps that is why the old sinner who narrates these tales, and who, like Gigi's Aunt Alicia, is so rich in erotic wisdom, has been the writer most widely revered and remembered. Colette escapes from war, old age, and debility into an innocent and lighthearted past. She reveals the smiling face she begrudged the camera throughout her life, and the maternal tenderness that she feared so terribly to show her child. They signal a sickbed conversion of sorts. It's not quite to a solid faith in love, in lasting happiness, or in redemption—Colette was too inveterate an unbeliever and too vigilant an artist to let herself go so far. But she allows that in an affair of the heart there may be no victims, and that lust may coexist with devotion.

Maurice Goudeket survived a six-week internment in the concentration camp at Compiègne, and Colette's reputation survived her ambiguous collaboration with the Occupation press. (Indeed, one feels she would have collaborated with the Devil himself to ensure the survival of the being most essential to her—the man she called "my best friend.") In 1945, she was elected to the Académie Goncourt—the second woman member in its history—and in 1949 her *confrères* chose her as their president.

After the liberation of Paris, Colette had ten years left. She spent most of them on the daybed she called her "raft," where she worked and slept. Her reading lamp had an improvised shade made of her blue writing paper. At night it marked her window to anyone passing through the Palais-Royal gardens. She would call her last memoir *Le Fanal bleu (The Blue Lantern)*.

Age, corpulence, and unremitting pain forced Colette to give up vagabondage, and she says that she renounced "egotism." But she could never renounce coquetry, and she could never "learn how not to write." "Perhaps the most praiseworthy thing about me," she concluded in an interview with Glenway Wescott two years before she died, "is that I have known how to write like a woman, without anything moralistic or theoretical, without promulgating." And by the end of the woman's story that

Colette spins as she lives, she is unbeholden to the gods of men.

MY MOTHER'S HOUSE and *SIDO*

Literature offers writers, as motherhood offers women, an opportunity to recover and repair the "dropped stitches" of a life, as Colette calls them, by creating an experience of wholeness for their readers or their children and, ultimately, for themselves. The expression for a dropped stitch is, in French, or at least in the provincial French Colette spoke as a girl, *une manque*, which also means a lack, a loss, or a deficiency. Writing *My Mother's House* was a profoundly reparative act in which, as Colette puts it, "the personage of my mother—the personage who has dominated all the rest of my work"—is placed at the heart of it.

In the autumn of 1921, Colette had taken her teenage stepson and lover, Bertrand de Jouvenel, on a sentimental journey to her birthplace, Saint-Sauveur-en-Puisaye. She had been reminiscing to the boy about her village girlhood, and he had seized upon these Balzacian recollections as the pretext for a little critical and moral lecture. Why, he asked, was she so fixated upon the louche characters she had depicted in *Chéri*, who had "so little interest,' when she could write about a fine subject that was compelling "in such a different fashion"?

Colette was obviously not unmoved by Bertrand's desire to rehabilitate her, coinciding, as it did so charmingly, with his desire to be corrupted by her. After their visit, she set to work on the autobiographical sketches that would comprise *My Mother's House*, telling an interviewer that her aim was to discover "her childhood, the real one; her adolescence, the reality of it, and then her mother. She would rediscover her, but this time it would be the good one." The chapters of her memoir were serialized in *Le Matin* and several other periodicals before being collected into a volume published by Ferenczi in 1922 with a title—*La Maison de Claudine*—that was a shameless commercial ploy. There is no reference in any of the vignettes—thirty in the original edition, twenty-nine in the present one—to the heroine of Colette's first novels.

Seven years elapsed between the publication of *My Mother's House* and its companion, *Sido*. (The definitive edition was published by Ferenczi in 1930, although an abbreviated version, entitled *Sido et les points cardinaux*, had appeared the previous year.) In her preface, Colette notes that "any writer whose existence is long drawn out turns in the end toward his past, either to revile it or to rejoice in it." What's striking about this explanation is the starkness of the choice—the triage, as Colette sees it—that the aging writer makes among her memories of childhood. The tone of her prose in *Sido* is elegiac and the scenes are suffused with a mellow, sentimental light. This memoir fulfills Colette's promise to her friend, the society confessor and diarist, abbé Mugnier, to write a book that would be a veritable "orgy of virtue."

Sido is constructed in three long sections which form a kind of memorial triptych. One is devoted to Colette's mother, one to her father, and one to her siblings. A tenderness born of her own maturity and happiness, as well as an experience of belated mourning, color the romantic portrait she gives of their characters. The truth also has its place, or *Sido* wouldn't be the persuasive, enduring work that it is. There are shadows of the disappointment and failure that haunted all of the Robineaus and Colettes—except, perhaps, the one who escaped to tell their tale. But "to look happy," she writes of her family, "was the highest compliment we paid one another." And that is the compliment which, in this memoir filled with pride and felicity, she pays them.

PREFACE

Between the appearance of *My Mother's House* and *Sido*, there was an interval of seven years. Looking back on those years, it does not seem to me that I found them long. This was because, by continually laying aside and taking up again the various short pieces which went to make up first *My Mother's House*, then *Sido*, I always remained in touch with the personage who, little by little, has dominated all the rest of my work: the personage of my mother. It haunts me still. The reasons for this prevailing presence are not far to seek: any writer whose existence is long drawn out turns in the end towards his past, either to revile it or rejoice in it. As a child I was poor and happy, like many children who need neither money nor comfort to achieve an active sort of happiness. But my felicity knew another and less commonplace secret: the presence of her who, instead of receding far from me through the gates of death, has revealed herself more vividly to me as I grow older. Ever since *Sido* appeared, this short form of her Christian name has starred all my memoirs. *La Naissance du Jour* gave me the chance to glorify her letters and boast of them. In *L'Etoile Vesper* it is to her I sometimes turn for a youthful touch—though my laugh, now that I am in the seventies, is not so gay as Sido's humour was when she mocked at the little tombstones of burnished lead and beads, and their rural epitaphs.

I am not at all sure that I have put the finishing touches to these portraits of her; nor am I at all sure that I have discovered all that she has bequeathed to me. I have come late to this task. But where could I find a better one for my last?

Colette.

MY MOTHER'S HOUSE

Translated by

UNA VICENZO TROUBRIDGE
and ENID MCLEOD

CONTENTS

WHERE ARE THE CHILDREN?

THE house was large, topped by a lofty garret. The steep gradient of the street compelled the coach-houses, stables, and poultry-house, the laundry and the dairy, to huddle on a lower level all round a closed courtyard.

By leaning over the garden wall, I could scratch with my finger the poultry-house roof. The Upper Garden overlooked the Lower Garden—a warm, confined enclosure reserved for the cultivation of aubergines and pimentos—where the smell of tomato leaves mingled in July with that of the apricots ripening on the walls. In the Upper Garden were two twin firs, a walnut-tree whose intolerant shade killed any flowers beneath it, some rose-bushes, a neglected lawn and a dilapidated arbour. At the bottom, along the Rue des Vignes, a boundary wall reinforced with a strong iron railing ought to have ensured the privacy of the two gardens, but I never knew those railings other than twisted and torn from their cement foundations, and grappling in mid air with the invincible arms of a hundred-year-old wistaria.

In the Rue de l'Hospice, a two-way flight of steps led up to the front door in the gloomy façade with its large bare windows. It was the typical burgher's house in an old village, but its dignity was upset a little by the steep gradient of the street, the stone steps being lopsided, ten on one side and six on the other.

A large solemn house, rather forbidding, with its shrill bell and its carriage-entrance with a huge bolt like an ancient dungeon, a house that smiled only on its garden side. The back, invisible to passers-by, was a sun-trap,

swathed in a mantle of wistaria and bignonia too heavy
for the trellis of worn iron-work, which sagged in the
middle like a hammock and provided shade for the little
flagged terrace and the threshold of the sitting-room.

Is it worth while, I wonder, seeking for adequate words
to describe the rest? I shall never be able to conjure up the
splendour that adorns, in my memory, the ruddy festoons
of an autumn vine borne down by its own weight and
clinging despairingly to some branch of the fir-trees.
And the massive lilacs, whose compact flowers—blue
in the shade and purple in the sunshine—withered so
soon, stifled by their own exuberance. The lilacs long
since dead will not be revived at my bidding, any more
than the terrifying moonlight—silver, quick-silver,
leaden-grey, with facets of dazzling amethyst or scintillat-
ing points of sapphire—all depending on a certain pane in
the blue glass window of the summer-house at the bottom
of the garden.

Both house and garden are living still, I know; but
what of that, if the magic has deserted them? If the secret
is lost that opened to me a whole world—light, scents,
birds and trees in perfect harmony, the murmur of
human voices now silent for ever—a world of which I
have ceased to be worthy?

It would happen sometimes long ago, when this house
and garden harboured a family, that a book lying open
on the flagstones of the terrace or on the grass, a skipping-
rope twisted like a snake across the path, or perhaps a
miniature garden, pebble-edged and planted with decap-
itated flowers, revealed both the presence of children and
their varying ages. But such evidence was hardly ever
accompanied by childish shouts or laughter, and my home,
though warm and full, bore an odd resemblance to those
houses which, once the holidays have come to an end,

are suddenly emptied of joy. The silence, the muted breeze of the enclosed garden, the pages of the book stirred only by invisible fingers, all seemed to be asking, "Where are the children?"

It was then, from beneath the ancient iron trellis sagging to the left under the wistaria, that my mother would make her appearance, small and plump in those days when age had not yet wasted her. She would scan the thick green clumps and, raising her head, fling her call into the air: "Children! Where are the children?"

Where indeed? Nowhere. My mother's cry would ring through the garden, striking the great wall of the barn and returning to her as a faint exhausted echo. "Where . . . ? Children . . . ?"

Nowhere. My mother would throw back her head and gaze heavenwards, as though waiting for a flock of winged children to alight from the skies. After a moment she would repeat her call; then, grown tired of questioning the heavens, she would crack a dry poppy-head with her finger-nail, rub the greenfly from a rose shoot, fill her pockets with unripe walnuts, and return to the house shaking her head over the vanished children.

And all the while, from among the leaves of the walnut-tree above her, gleamed the pale, pointed face of a child who lay stretched like a tom-cat along a big branch, and never uttered a word. A less short-sighted mother might well have suspected that the spasmodic salutations exchanged by the twin tops of the two firs were due to some influence other than that of the sudden October squalls! And in the square dormer, above the pulley for hauling up fodder, would she not have perceived, if she had screwed up her eyes, two pale patches among the hay —the face of a young boy and the pages of his book?

But she had given up looking for us, had despaired of

trying to reach us. Our uncanny turbulence was never accompanied by any sound. I do not believe there can ever have been children so active and so mute. Looking back at what we were, I am amazed. No one had imposed upon us either our cheerful silence or our limited sociability. My nineteen-year-old brother, engrossed in constructing some hydrotherapeutic apparatus out of linen bladders, strands of wire and glass tubes, never prevented the younger, aged fourteen, from disembowelling a watch or from transposing on the piano, with never a false note, a melody or an air from a symphony heard at a concert in the county town. He did not even interfere with his junior's incomprehensible passion for decorating the garden with little tombstones cut out of cardboard, and each inscribed, beneath the sign of the cross, with the names, epitaph, and genealogy of the imaginary person deceased.

My sister with the too long hair might read for ever with never a pause; the two boys would brush past her as though they did not see the young girl sitting abstracted and entranced, and never bother her. When I was small, I was at liberty to keep up as best I could with my long-legged brothers as they ranged the woods in pursuit of swallow tails, White Admirals, Purple Emperors, or hunted for grass snakes, or gathered armfuls of the tall July foxgloves which grew in the clearings already aglow with patches of purple heather. But I followed them in silence, picking blackberries, bird-cherries, a chance wild flower, or roving the hedgerows and waterlogged meadows like an independent dog out hunting on its own.

"Where are the children?" She would suddenly appear like an over-solicitous mother-bitch breathlessly pursuing her constant quest, head lifted and scenting the breeze.

Sometimes her white linen sleeves bore witness that she had come from kneading dough for cakes or making the pudding that had a velvety hot sauce of rum and jam. If she had been washing the Havanese bitch, she would be enveloped in a long blue apron, and sometimes she would be waving a banner of rustling yellow paper, the paper used round the butcher's meat, which meant that she hoped to reassemble, at the same time as her elusive children, her carnivorous family of vagabond cats.

To her traditional cry she would add, in the same anxious and appealing key, a reminder of the time of day. "Four o'clock, and they haven't come in to tea! Where are the children? . . ." "Half-past six! Will they come home to dinner? Where are the children? . . ." That lovely voice; how I should weep for joy if I could hear it now! Our only sin, our single misdeed, was silence, and a kind of miraculous vanishing. For perfectly innocent reasons, for the sake of a liberty that no one denied us, we clambered over the railing, leaving behind our shoes, and returned by way of an unnecessary ladder or a neighbour's low wall.

Our anxious mother's keen sense of smell would discover on us traces of wild garlic from a distant ravine or of marsh mint from a treacherous bog. The dripping pocket of one of the boys would disgorge the bathing slip worn in malarial ponds, and the "little one", cut about the knees and skinned at the elbows, would be bleeding complacently under plasters of cobweb and wild pepper bound on with rushes.

"To-morrow I shall keep you locked up! All of you, do you hear, every single one of you!"

To-morrow! Next day the eldest, slipping on the slated roof where he was fitting a tank, broke his collar-bone and remained at the foot of the wall waiting, politely silent and half unconscious, until someone came to pick him up. Next day an eighteen-rung ladder crashed plumb on the forehead of the younger son, who never uttered a cry, but brought home with becoming modesty a lump like a purple egg between his eyes.

"Where are the children?"

Two are at rest. The others grow older day by day. If there be a place of waiting after this life, then surely she who so often waited for us has not ceased to tremble for those two who are yet alive.

For the eldest of us all, at any rate, she has done with looking at the dark window pane every evening and saying, "I feel that child is not happy. I feel she is suffering." And for the elder of the boys she no longer listens, breathlessly, to the wheels of a doctor's trap coming over the snow at night, or to the hoof beats of the grey mare.

But I know that for the two who remain she seeks and wanders still, invisible, tormented by her inability to watch over them enough.

"Where, oh where are the children? . . ."

THE SAVAGE

SHE was eighteen years old when, in about 1853, he carried her off from her family, consisting of two brothers only, French journalists married and settled in Belgium, and from her friends—painters, musicians and poets—an entire Bohemia of young French and Belgian artists. A fair-haired girl, not particularly pretty, but attractive, with a wide mouth, a pointed chin and humorous grey eyes, and her hair gathered into a precarious knot slipping from its hairpins at the nape of her neck. An emancipated girl, accustomed to the frank companionship of boys, her brothers and their friends. A dowerless young woman, without trousseau or jewels, but with a slender supple body above her voluminous skirts: a young woman with a neat waist and softly rounded shoulders, small and sturdy.

The Savage saw her on a summer's day while she was spending a few weeks with her peasant foster-mother on a visit from Belgium to France, and when he was visiting his neighbouring estates on horseback. Accustomed to his servant-girls, easy conquests as easily forsaken, his mind dwelt upon this unselfconscious young woman who had returned his glance, unsmiling and unabashed. The passing vision of this man on his strawberry roan, with his youthful black beard and romantic pallor, was not unpleasing to the young woman, but by the time he had learned her name she had already forgotten him. He was told that they called her "Sido", short for Sidonie. A stickler for formalities, as are so many "savages", he resorted to lawyers and relations, and her family in

Belgium were informed that this scion of gentlemen glass-blowers possessed farms and forest land, a country house with a garden, and ready money enough. Sido listened, scared and silent, rolling her fair curls round her fingers. But when a young girl is without fortune or profession, and is, moreover, entirely dependent on her brothers, what can she do but hold her tongue, accept what is offered and thank God for it?

So she quitted the warm Belgian house and the vaulted kitchen that smelled of gas, new bread and coffee; she left behind the piano, the violin, the big Salvator Rosa inherited from her father, the tobacco-jar and the long, slender clay pipes, the coke braziers, the open books and crumpled newspapers, and, as a young bride, she entered the country house isolated during the hard winters in that forest land.

There she discovered an unexpected drawing-room, all white and gold, on the ground floor, but an upper storey barely rough-cast and as deserted as a loft. In the stables a pair of good horses and a couple of cows ate their fill of hay and corn; butter was churned and cheeses manufactured in the outbuildings; but the bedrooms were icy and suggested neither love nor sweet sleep.

Family silver engraved with a goat rampant, cut glass, and wine were there in abundance. In the evenings, by candlelight, shadowy old women sat spinning in the kitchen, stripping and winding flax grown on the estate to make heavy cold linen, impossible to wear out, for beds and household use. The shrill cackle of truculent kitchenmaids rose and fell, depending on their master's approach or departure; bearded old witches cast malign glances upon the young bride, and a handsome laundry-maid, discarded by the squire, leaned against the well, filling the air with noisy lamentations whenever the Savage was out hunting.

The Savage—a well-intentioned fellow in the main—began by being kind to his civilised little bride. But Sido, who longed for friends, for innocent and cheerful company, encountered in her own home no one but servants, cautious farmers, and gamekeepers reeking of wine and the blood of hares, who left a smell of wolves behind them. To these the Savage spoke seldom and always with arrogance. Descendant of a once noble family, he had inherited their disdain, their courtesy, their brutality, and their taste for the society of inferiors. His nickname referred exclusively to his unsociable habit of riding alone, of hunting without dog or companion, and to his taciturnity. Sido was a lover of conversation, of persiflage, of variety, of despotic and loving kindness and of all gentleness. She filled the great house with flowers, whitewashed the dark kitchen, personally superintended the cooking of Flemish dishes, baked rich plum cakes and longed for the birth of her first child. The Savage would put in a brief appearance between two excursions, smile at her and be gone once more. He would be off to his vineyards, to his swampy forests, loitering long at the wayside inns where, except for one tall candle, all is dark: the rafters, the smoke-blackened walls, the rye bread and the metal tankards filled with wine.

Having come to the end of her epicurean recipes, her furniture polish and her patience, Sido, wasted by loneliness, wept; and the Savage perceived the traces of tears that she denied. He realised confusedly that she was bored, that she was feeling the lack of some kind of comfort and luxury alien to his melancholy. What could it be?

One morning he set off on horseback, trotted forty miles to the county town, swooped down upon its shops

and returned the following night carrying, with a fine air
of awkward ostentation, two surprising objects destined
for the delight and delectation of his young wife: a
little mortar of rarest marble, for pounding almonds and
sweetmeats, and a cashmere shawl.

I can if I like still make almond paste with sugar and
lemon peel in the now cracked and dingy mortar, but I
reproach myself for having cut up the cherry-coloured
shawl to make cushion covers and vanity bags. For my
mother, who had been in her youth the unloving and
uncomplaining Sido of her first and saturnine husband,
cherished both shawl and mortar with sentimental care.

"You see," she would say to me, "the Savage, who had
never known how to give, did bring them to me. He
took a lot of trouble to bring them to me, tied to the
saddle of his mare, Mustapha. He stood before me
holding them in his arms, as proud and clumsy as a big
dog with a small slipper in his mouth. And I realised
there and then that in his eyes his presents were not just a
mortar and a shawl. They were "Presents", rare and
costly things that he had gone a long way to find; it was
his first unselfish effort—and his last, poor soul—to
amuse and comfort a lonely young exile who was
weeping."

JEALOUSY

"THERE's nothing for dinner to-night. Tricotet hadn't yet killed this morning. He was going to kill at noon. I'm going myself to the butcher's, just as I am. What a nuisance! Why should one have to eat? And what shall we eat this evening?"

My mother stands, utterly discouraged, by the window. She is wearing her house frock of spotted sateen, her silver brooch with twin angels encircling the portrait of a child, her spectacles on a chain and her lorgnette suspended from a black silk cord that catches on every door key, breaks on every drawer handle, and has been reknotted a score of times. She looks at each of us in turn, hopelessly. She is well aware that not one of us will make a useful suggestion. If appealed to, my father will reply, "Raw tomatoes with plenty of pepper."

"Red cabbage and vinegar," would have been the contribution of my elder brother, Achille, whose medical studies keep him in Paris.

My second brother, Léo, will ask for "A big bowl of chocolate!" and I, bounding into the air because I so often forget that I am past fifteen, will clamour for "Fried potatoes! Fried potatoes! And walnuts with cheese!"

It appears, however, that fried potatoes, chocolate, tomatoes and red cabbage do not constitute "a dinner".

"But why, mother?"

"Don't ask foolish questions!"

She is absorbed in her problem. She has already seized hold of the black cane basket with a double lid and is about to set forth, just as she is, wearing her wide-brimmed garden hat, scorched by three summers, its little crown banded with a dark brown ruche, and her gardening apron, in one pocket of which the curved beak of her secateur has poked a hole. Some dry love-in-the-mist seeds in a twist of paper in the bottom of the other pocket make a sound like rain and finger-nails scratching silk as she walks.

In my vanity on her behalf, I cry out after her, "Mother, do take off your apron!"

Without stopping, she turns towards me that face, framed by its bands of hair, which looks its full fifty-five years when she is sad and when she is gay would still pass for thirty.

"Why on earth? I'm only going to the Rue de la Roche."

"Can't you leave your mother alone?" grumbles my father into his beard. "By the way, where is she going?"

"To Léonore's, for the dinner."

"Aren't you going with her?"

"No. I don't feel like it to-day."

There are days when Léonore's shop, with its knives, its hatchet, and its bulging bullocks' lungs, pink as the pulpy flesh of a begonia, iridescent as they sway in the breeze, delight me as much as would a confectioner's. Léonore cuts me a slice of salted bacon and hands me the transparent rasher between the tips of her cold fingers. In the butcher's garden, Marie Tricotet, though born on the same day as myself, still derives amusement from pricking the unemptied bladders of pigs or calves and treading on them to "make a fountain". The horrid sound of skin being torn from newly killed flesh, the roundness of kidneys—brown fruit nestling in immaculate padding of rosy lard—arouse in me a complicated repugnance that attracts me while I do my best to hide it. But the delicate fat that remains in the hollow of the little cloven pig's trotter when the heat of the fire bursts it open, that I eat as a wholesome delicacy! No matter. To-day, I have no wish to follow my mother.

My father does not insist, but hoists himself nimbly on to his one leg, grasps his crutch and his stick, and goes upstairs to the library. Before going, he meticulously folds the newspaper, *Le Temps*, hides it under the cushion of his armchair, and thrusts the bright blue-covered *La Nature* into the pocket of his long overcoat. His small Cossack eye, gleaming beneath an eyebrow of hempen grey, takes the table for printed provender which will vanish to the library and be seen no more. But we, well trained in this little game, have left him nothing to take.

"You've not seen the *Mercure de France*?"

"No, father."

"Nor the *Revue Bleue*?"

"No, father."

He glares at his children with the eyes of an inquisitor.

"I should like to know who it is, in this house, who . . ."

He relieves his feelings in gloomy and impersonal conjecture, embellished with venemous expletives. His house has become *this* house, a domain of disorder, wherein *these* "base-born" children profess contempt for the written word, encouraged, moreover, by *that* woman. . . .

"Which reminds me, where is that woman now?"

"Why, she's gone to Léonore's, father."

"Again?"

"But she's only just started. . . ."

He pulls out his watch, consults it as though he were going to bed and, for want of anything better, grabs a two-day-old copy of *L'Office de Publicité* before going up to the library. With his right hand he keeps a firm grip

on the cross-piece of the crutch that acts as a prop for his
right armpit: in his other he has only a stick. As it dies
away, I listen to that firm, regular rhythm of two sticks
and a single foot, which has soothed me all my childhood.
But suddenly, to-day, a new uneasiness assails me, because
for the first time I have noticed the prominent veins and
wrinkles on my father's strikingly white hands, and
how the fringe of thick hair at the nape of his neck has
faded just lately. Can it really be true that he will soon be
sixty years old?

It is cool and melancholy on the front steps, where
I wait for my mother's return. At last I hear the sound
of her neat little footsteps in the Rue de la Roche, and
I am surprised at how happy it makes me feel. She
comes round the corner and down the hill towards me,
preceded by the dog—the horror from Patason's—and
she is in a hurry.

"Let me pass, darling! If I don't give this shoulder of
mutton to Henriette to roast at once, we shall dine off
shoe-leather. Where's your father?"

I follow her, vaguely disturbed for the first time that
she should be worrying about my father. Since she left
him only half an hour ago and he scarcely ever goes out,
she knows perfectly well where he is. There would have
been more sense, for instance, had she said to me, "Minet-
Chéri, you're looking pale. Minet-Chéri, what's the
matter?"

Without replying, I watch her throw off her old garden
hat with a youthful gesture that reveals her grey hair and
her face, fresh coloured, but marked here and there with
ineffaceable lines. Is it possible—why, yes, after all, I am
the youngest of us four—is it possible that my mother
is nearly fifty-four? I never think about it. I should like
to forget it.

Here comes the man on whom her thoughts are centred.
Here he comes, bristling, his beard tilted aggressively. He
has been listening for the bang of the closing front door,
he has come down from his eyrie.

"There you are! You've taken your time about it."

She turns on him, quick as a cat.

"Taken my time? Are you trying to be funny? I've
simply been there and come straight back."

"Back from where? From Léonore's?"

"Of course not. I had to go to Corneau's for . . ."

"For his sheep's eyes? And his comments on the
weather?"

"Don't be tiresome! Then I had to go and get the black-
currant tea at Cholet's."

The small Cossack eye darts a piercing look.

"Ah, ha! At Cholet's!"

My father throws his head back and runs his hand
through his thick hair that is almost white.

"Ah, ha! At Cholet's! And did you happen to notice
that he's losing his hair and that you can see his pate?"

"No. I didn't notice it."

"You didn't notice it? No, of course not! You were
far too busy making eyes at the popinjays having a drink
at the café opposite, and at Mabilat's two sons!"

"Oh! This is too much! I, I making eyes at Mabilat's
sons! Upon my word, I don't know how you dare! I
swear to you I didn't even turn my head in the direction of
his place. And the proof of that is . . ."

Indignantly my mother folds her hands, pretty still
though ageing and weatherbeaten, over a bosom held up by
gusseted stays. Blushing beneath the bands of her greying
hair, her chin trembling with resentment, this little elderly
lady is charming when she defends herself without so
much as a smile against the accusations of a jealous

sexagenarian. Nor does he smile either, as he goes on to accuse her now of "gallivanting". But I can still smile at their quarrels because I am only fifteen, and have not yet divined the ferocity of love beneath his veteran eyebrow, and the blushes of adolescence upon her fading cheeks.

THE LITTLE ONE

A SMELL of crushed grass hangs over the unmown lawn, where the lush new blades lie trodden in all directions by the children's games, as if laid flat by a heavy shower of hail. Fierce little heels have dug into the paths and scattered gravel over the flower beds; a skipping-rope dangles from the pump handle; dolls' plates the size of marguerites star the grass; and a long feline wail of boredom heralds the close of day, the cats' awakening and the approach of dinner-time.

The Little One's playmates have only just left her. Disdaining the door, they have jumped over the railing at the bottom of the garden, hurling their final frenzied yells into the deserted Rue des Vignes, screaming their childish oaths with uncouth shrugs of the shoulders, straddling, contorting their features into diabolical squints and froglike grimaces, and putting out their tongues stained with violet ink. On the other side of the wall, the Little One—otherwise known as Minet-Chéri—has mustered her remaining stock of heavy mockery, loud laughter and country slang to hurl in pursuit of them. The voices of these little girls had been hoarse, their eyes and cheeks ablaze, as though they had been given some intoxicant to drink. Now they have gone away exhausted, as though this whole afternoon devoted to games had debased them. There was neither idleness nor boredom to ennoble in some sort the overlong and degrading pursuit of pleasure, which left the Little One looking sick and plainer than usual.

Sundays are sometimes empty days of idle dreaming: white shoes and starched dresses are not conducive to the wilder forms of frenzy. But Thursday, with its rabble of unemployed, on strike in black pinafores and hobnailed boots, Thursday permits of all and everything. For nearly five hours these children have tasted the full licence of Thursday. One of them has played at being the invalid, another has sold coffee to a third, a horse-dealer, who in return has sold her a cow. "Thirty louis and a gift at that! Swine to you if you say it isn't!" Jeanne has got inside the skin of Grandpapa Gruel, the dealer in tripe and rabbit-skins, while Yvonne has impersonated his lean daughter, a wretched and dissolute hag. Scire and his wife, Gruel's neighbours, have looked out through the eyes of Gabrielle and Sandrine, and all the filth of a squalid village street has poured forth from six childish mouths. Hideous tittle-tattle of rascally and low love-life has disfigured lips, stained with cherry juice, on which a trace of teatime honey still glistened.

One of them pulled a pack of cards from her pocket and cries broke out. And had not three of the six little girls already learned to cheat, adepts at licking their thumbs in pot-house style and slamming down a trump on the table with a: "Trumpety-trump! You've scraped the bottom of the barrel and you haven't scored a single trick!" Not a single event of village life that they have not declaimed and mimicked with passionate intensity! This Thursday has been one of those shunned by Minet-Chéri's mother, who has retreated fearfully into the house, as though before an invading army.

And now all is silence in the garden. First one cat, then two more, stretch and yawn before extending a doubtful paw to test the gravel path, just as they do after a storm. They set off towards the house, and the Little One, having started to follow them, pauses: she does not feel worthy. She will wait until her normal pallor, like an inner dawn that celebrates the departure of evil demons, rises again into her hot cheeks still dark with over-excitement. She opens her wide mouth for a final shout, showing her recently cut eye-teeth. She opens her eyes to the full, wrinkles her forehead, gives vent to a "pouf" of exhaustion, and wipes her nose on the back of her hand.

A school pinafore envelops her like a sack from neck to knees, and her hair, after the fashion of poor children, is looped in two plaits behind her ears. What will become of her hands, clawed and scratched by cats and brambles, or of her feet laced into boots of light brown kid? There are days when they say that the Little One will be pretty later on. To-day she is ugly, and feels upon her face the passing ugliness of her perspiration, the marks of dirty fingers on her cheek and, above all, the successive mimicries that have linked her with Jeanne, with Sandrine, with Aline, the daily dressmaker, with the chemist's wife and the postmaster's daughter. For the children had crowned the afternoon's sport with a long game of "What shall we be when we're grown up?"

"When I'm grown up, I shall . . ."

Though such skilled mimics, they lack imagination. A sort of resigned wisdom, the peasant terror of adventure and distant travel, already keeps them all—the clockmaker's child, the grocer's little girl and the offspring of the butcher and the laundress—chained to their parents' shops.

It is true that Jeanne roundly announced, "I shall be a tart!"

"But that sort of thing," Minet-Chéri reflects contemptuously, "is simply childish nonsense."

Having no special wish when her turn came, she had thrown out with a certain contempt, "I? Oh, I shall be a sailor!" And that was simply because she sometimes dreamed of being a boy, and wearing trousers and a blue beret. The sea, of which Minet-Chéri knows nothing, the ship breasting a wave, the golden island and the gleaming fruit, all that only surged up much later, to serve as a background to the blue blouse and the cap with a pompom.

"I shall be a sailor, and on my voyages . . ."

She sits down on the grass to rest and reflect. Travel? Adventure? For a child who, twice a year, at the periods of the great spring and winter provisioning, leaves the confines of her district, and drives in a victoria to her county town, such words have neither force nor value. They evoke only the printed page, the coloured picture. The Little One, now very tired, repeats the words "When I go round the world . . ." automatically, just as she would say, "When I go gathering chestnuts . . ."

In the house a lamp behind the sitting-room window suddenly glows red and the Little One shivers. All that had looked green up to the moment before, now turns blue around this motionless red flame. The child's hand, trailing in the grass, is suddenly aware of the evening damp. It is the hour of lamps. Leaves rustle together with a sound like the plash of running water and the door of the hayloft flaps against the wall as it does in a winter gale. The garden, grown suddenly hostile, menaces a now sobered little girl with the cold leaves of its laurels, the raised sabres of its yuccas, and the barbed caterpillars of its monkey-puzzle tree. A roar like the ocean comes from the direction of Moutiers where the wind, unchecked, runs in flurries over the tossing tree-tops. The Little One, sitting on the grass, keeps her eyes fixed on the lamp, veiled for a moment by a brief eclipse. A hand has passed in front of the flame, a hand wearing a shining thimble. At the mere sight of this hand the Little One starts to her feet, pale, gentle now, trembling slightly as a child must who for the first time ceases to be the happy little vampire that unconsciously drains the maternal heart; trembling slightly at the conscious realisation that this hand and this flame, and the bent, anxious head beside the lamp, are the centre and the secret birthplace whence radiate in ripples ever less perceptible, in circles ever more and more remote from the essential light and its vibrations, the warm sitting-room with its flora of cut branches and its fauna of peaceful creatures; the echoing house, dry, warm and crackling as a newly-baked loaf; the garden, the village. . . . Beyond these all is danger, all is loneliness.

The "sailor", with faltering steps, ventures upon *terra firma* and makes for the house, turning her back on an enormous yellow moon, just rising. Adventure? Travels? The enterprise that makes the emigrant? With her eyes glued to the shining thimble, to the hand that passes to and fro before the flame, Minet-Chéri savours the delicious contrition of being—like the clockmaker's child, like the little girls of the laundress and the baker—a child of her village, hostile alike to colonist and barbarian, one of those whose universe is bounded by the limits of a field, by the entrance of a shop, by the circle of light spreading beneath a lamp and crossed at intervals by a well-loved hand drawing a thread and wearing a silver thimble.

THE ABDUCTION

"I CAN'T go on living like this!" exclaimed my mother. "Last night I dreamed again that you were being kidnapped. Three times I climbed the stairs to your door, and I got no sleep at all."

I looked at her with compassion, for she seemed both tired and anxious. I said nothing, however, as I knew of no cure for her anxiety.

"And is that all you care about it, little monstress?"

"Well, hang it all, mother! What do you want me to say? You look as though you blamed me for its being only a dream."

She raised her arms to heaven, and ran to the door. As she went she caught the cord of her pince-nez round the key of a drawer, then the ribbon of her lorgnette in the latch of the door, and entangled her knitted shawl in the gothic intricacies of a Second Empire chair. Repressing half an oath, she disappeared with an indignant glance at me, murmuring: "Nine years old! . . . And that's how she answers me when I speak of serious matters!"

My half-sister's marriage had recently left me in possession of her bedroom, the room on the first floor, starred with cornflowers upon a pearl-grey background.

Deserting my childhood's lair—formerly a porter's den, with huge beams and a tiled floor, perched over the carriage entrance and communicating with my mother's bedroom—I had been sleeping for four weeks in the bed that I had never even dared to covet, the bed whose white lace curtains lined with pitiless blue were held back by rosettes of burnished lead. The little cupboard-dressing-room belonged to me too, and I could lean out of each of the windows with simulated melancholy and disdain at the hour when the small Blancvillains and the Trinitets passed by, gnawing their tea-time slices of bread liberally piled with red beans pickled in wine sauce.

At every opportunity I would say, "I'm going up to my room . . . Céline has left the shutters in my room open."

But my happiness was threatened: my mother was anxious and ever on the watch. Since my sister's marriage she was one child short, and at that time the front pages of the newspapers carried the picture of some young girl or other who had been abducted and kept in hiding. A tramp, refused admittance by our cook as night was falling, had refused to go away and stuck his stick in the jamb of the door until my father arrived on the scene. Finally some gipsies, encountered on the road, had offered with flashing smiles and looks of ill-concealed hatred to buy my hair; and M. Demange, an old gentleman who never spoke to anyone, had unbent so far as to offer me comfits from his snuffbox.

"None of which is really very serious," my father assured my mother.

"Oh, you! So long as no one interferes with your after-luncheon cigarette and your game of dominoes, you don't even stop to think that nowadays the Little One sleeps upstairs, and that a staircase, the dining-room, a passage and the sitting-room lie between her and my bedroom. I've had enough of this perpetual anxiety over my daughters. Already the eldest has gone off with that man. . . ."

"How, gone off?"

"Oh, well, married him if you prefer it. Married or not

married, she has none the less gone away with a man whom she hardly knows."

She gave my father a look of loving suspicion.

"And after all, you, what have you to do with me? You aren't even a relation!"

During mealtimes I revelled in the veiled allusions, couched in the language so dear to parents, wherein an enigmatic term replaces the word in common use, and in which pursed lips and dramatic throat-clearings attract and rivet the attention of children.

"At Ghent, when I was young," my mother would relate, "one of our friends who was only sixteen was abducted—she was indeed! And, what's more, in a carriage and pair! The next day . . . Well . . . hum . . . naturally! There could be no question of returning her to her family. There are some—how shall I put it?—some breaches . . . In the end they got married. There was no other way out."

"There was no other way out."

Imprudent words! A small old-fashioned engraving, hanging in a dark passage, suddenly interested me. It represented a post-chaise, harnessed to two queer horses with necks like fabulous beasts'. In front of the gaping coach door a young man, dressed in taffeta, was carrying on one arm with the greatest of ease a fainting young woman. Her little mouth forming an O, and the ruffled petticoats framing her charming legs, strove to express extreme terror. "*The Abduction!*" My innocent imagination was pleasantly stirred by the word and the picture.

One windy night, when the loose-fitting doors in the farmyard were banging and the loft was groaning over my head in the gusts that rushed in under the edges of the badly joined slates, sweeping it from west to east and

playing tunes like a wheezy mouth-organ, I was sleeping
soundly, worn out by a Thursday spent in the fields shaking down chestnuts and celebrating the brewing of the
new cider. Did I dream that my door creaked on its
hinges? So many hinges, so many weather-cocks were
creaking around me. Two arms, singularly adept at
lifting a sleeping form, encircled my waist and my neck,
at the same time gathering the blankets and the sheet
about me. My cheek felt the colder air of the stairs, a
muffled heavy step descended slowly, rocking me at each
pace with a gentle motion. Did I really wake? I doubt it.
Only a dream could waft a little girl right out of her childhood and place her, neither surprised nor unwilling, in the
very midst of a hypocritical and adventurous adolescence.
Only a dream could thus turn a loving child into the ungrateful creature that she will become to-morrow, the
crafty accomplice of the stranger, the forgetful one who
will leave her mother's house without a backward glance.
In such wise was I departing for the land where a post-
chaise, amid the jangling of bells, stops before a church to
deposit a young man dressed in taffeta and a young woman
whose ruffled skirts suggest the rifled petals of a rose. I did
not cry out. The two arms were so gentle, so careful to
hold me close enough to protect my dangling feet at every
doorway. A familiar rhythm actually seemed to lull me to
sleep in the abducting arms.

When day broke, I failed to recognise my old garret,
encumbered now with ladders and broken furniture,
whither my anxious mother had borne me in the night,
like a mother cat who secretly changes the hiding place of
her little one. Tired out, she slept, and awoke only when
the walls of my forgotten cell rang with my piercing
cry:

"Mother! Come quick! I've been abducted!"

THE PRIEST ON THE WALL

"WHAT are you thinking about, Bel-Gazou?"
"Nothing, mother."

An excellent answer. The same that I invariably gave when I was her age, and was known by the same name in the intimacy of my home. Whence comes the name and why did my father call me by it, long ago? No doubt it is the Provençal form of *beau gazouillis*—pretty prattle—but it would not disgrace the hero or the heroine of a Persian fairy tale.

"Nothing, mother." It is no bad thing that children should occasionally, and politely, put parents in their proper place. All temples are sacred. How dull and tactless I must sometimes seem to my Bel-Gazou of to-day! My question falls like a stone and cracks the magic mirror that reflects, surrounded by its favourite phantoms, the image of a child that I shall never see. I know that, in her father's eyes, my daughter is a kind of little female paladin who rules over her own lands, brandishing a hazel lance, cleaving haycocks, and driving the flock before her as though she were taking it on a crusade. I know that a smile from her enchants him, and that when he whispers, "Doesn't she look adorable just now?" it is because, at that particular moment, he sees on her childish features the amazing resemblance to a certain masculine face.

I know that to her faithful nurse, my Bel-Gazou is alternately the centre of the universe, a consummate masterpiece, a possessed monster from whom the devil must hourly be exorcised, a champion runner, a dizzy abyss of perversity, a *dear little one*[1] and a baby rabbit.

[1] These three words are in English in the original.

But who will tell me how my daughter appears to herself?

At her age—not quite eight years old—I was a priest on a wall, the thick high wall that divided the garden from the farmyard, and of which the flat tiled summit, broad as a pavement, served me as promenade and terrace, inaccessible to the ordinary run of mortals. Yes, I mean it; a priest on a wall. Why should it seem incredible? I was a priest without religious duties or parish, without any irreverent travesty, but none the less, unknown to all, a priest. A priest just as you, sir, happen to be bald, or you, madam, arthritic.

The word "presbytery" had chanced that year to drop into my sensitive ears and had wrought havoc.

"It's undoubtedly the most cheerful presbytery that I know of . . ." someone had said in my hearing.

Far from me the idea of asking one of my relations: "What kind of a thing is a presbytery?" I had absorbed the mysterious word with its harsh and spiky beginning and the brisk trot of its final syllables. Enriched by a secret and a doubt, I slept on the *word* and bore it off to my wall. "Presbytery!" I would shout it over the roof of the hen-house and Miton's garden, towards the perpetually misty horizon of Moutiers. From the summit of my wall, the word rang out as a malediction: "Begone! You are all presbyteries!" I shouted to invisible outlaws.

Later on the word lost some of its venom and I began to suspect that "presbytery" might very possibly be the scientific term for a certain little yellow-and-black striped snail. A chance remark was to be my undoing, in one of those moments wherein a child, however solemn or fanciful she may be, fleetingly resembles the picture made of her by grown-up people.

"Mother! Look what a lovely little presbytery I've found!"

"A lovely little . . . what?"

"A lovely little presb . . ."

I broke off, but too late. I had to learn—"I sometimes wonder if this child is all there"—that of which I was so anxious to remain in ignorance, and to "call things by their proper names. . . ."

"Come now, a presbytery is a priest's house."

"A priest's house. . . . Then Monsieur Millot, the priest, lives in a presbytery?"

"Why, of course he does. . . . Keep your mouth shut and breathe through your nose. . . . Of course he does. . . ."

I still tried to react. . . . I fought against the intrusion, closely hugging the tatters of my absurdity. I longed to compel Monsieur Millot, during my pleasure, to inhabit the empty shell of the little "presbytery" snail. . . .

"When will you learn to keep your mouth shut when you're not speaking? What are you thinking about?"

"Nothing, mother. . . ."

And then I yielded. I was craven and I compromised with my disappointment. Throwing away the fragments of the little broken snail shell, I picked up the enchanting word and, climbing on to my narrow terrace, shaded by the old lilac trees and adorned with polished pebbles and scraps of coloured glass like a thieving magpie's nest— I christened it the Presbytery and inducted myself as priest on the wall.

MY MOTHER AND THE BOOKS

THROUGH the open top of its shade, the lamp cast its beams upon a wall entirely corrugated by the backs of books, all bound. The opposite wall was yellow, the dirty yellow of the paper-backed volumes, read, re-read and in tatters. A few "Translated from the English" —price, one franc twenty-five—gave a scarlet note to the lowest shelf.

Halfway up, Musset, Voltaire and the Gospels gleamed in their leaf-brown sheepskin. Littré, Larousse and Becquerel displayed bulging backs like black tortoises, while d'Orbigny, pulled to pieces by the irreverent adoration of four children, scattered its pages blazoned with dahlias, parrots, pink-fringed jellyfish and duck-billed platypi.

Camille Flammarion, in gold-starred blue, contained the yellow planets, the chalk-white frozen craters of the moon, and Saturn rolling within his orbit like an iridescent pearl.

Two solid earth-coloured partitions held together Elisée Reclus, Voltaire in marbled boards, Balzac in black, and Shakespeare in olive-green.

After all these years, I have only to shut my eyes to see once more those walls faced with books. In those days I could find them in the dark. I never took a lamp when I went at night to choose one, it was enough to feel my way, as though on the keyboard of a piano, along the shelves. Lost, stolen or strayed, I could catalogue them to-day. Almost every one of them had been there before my birth.

There was a time, before I learned to read, when I would curl up into a ball, like a dog in its kennel, between two volumes of Larousse. Labiche and Daudet wormed their way early into my happy childhood, condescending teachers who played with a familiar pupil. Mérimée came along with them, seductive and severe, dazzling my eight years at times with an incomprehensible light. *Les Misérables* also, yes, *Les Misérables*—in spite of Gavroche; but that was a case of a reasoned passion which lived to weather coldness and long infidelities. No love lost between me and Dumas, save that the *Collier de la Reine* glittered for a few nights in my dreams upon the doomed neck of Jeanne de la Motte. Neither the enthusiasm of my brothers nor the disapproving surprise of my parents could persuade me to take an interest in the Musketeers.

There was never any question of my taste in children's books. Enamoured of the Princess in her chariot, dreaming beneath an attenuated crescent moon, and of Beauty sleeping in the wood surrounded by her prostrate pages; in love with Lord Puss in his gigantic funnel boots, I searched vainly in Perrault's text for the velvet blacks, the flash of silver, the ruins, the knights, the elegant little hooves of the horses of Gustave Doré; after a couple of pages I returned, disappointed, to Doré himself. I read the story of the Hind and that of Beauty only in Walter Crane's pure, fresh illustrations. The large characters of his text linked up picture with picture like the plain pieces of net connecting the patterns in lace. But not a single word ever passed the barrier that I erected against them. What becomes in later life of that tremendous determination not to know, that quiet strength expended on avoidance and rejection?

Books, books, books. It was not that I read so many. I read and re-read the same ones. But all of them were necessary to me. Their presence, their smell, the letters of their titles and the texture of their leather bindings. Perhaps those most hermetically sealed were the dearest. I have long forgotten the name of the author of a scarlet-clad Encyclopedia, but the alphabetical references marked upon each volume have remained for me an indelible and magic word: *Aphbicécladiggalhymaroidphorebstevanzy*. And how I loved the Guizot whose ornate green and gold was never opened! And the inviolate *Voyage d'Anacharsis!* If the *Histoire du Consulat et de l'Empire* ever found its way to the Quais, I wager that a label would proudly proclaim its condition as "mint".

The twenty-odd volumes of Saint-Simon replaced each other nightly at my mother's bedside; their pages provided her with endlessly renewed pleasure, and she thought it strange that at eight years old I should some-times fail to share in her enjoyment.

"Why don't you read Saint-Simon?" she would ask me. "I can't understand why children are so slow in learning to appreciate really interesting books!"

Beautiful books that I used to read, beautiful books that I left unread, warm covering of the walls of my home, variegated tapestry whose hidden design rejoiced my initiated eyes. It was from them I learned, long before the age for love, that love is complicated, tyrannical and even burdensome, since my mother grudged the prom-inence they gave it.

"It's a great bore—all the love in these books," she used to say. "In life, my poor Minet-Chéri, folk have other fish to fry. Did none of these lovesick people you read of have children to rear or a garden to care for? Judge for yourself, Minet-Chéri, have you or your brothers ever heard me harp on love as they do in books? And yet I think I ought to know something about it, having had two husbands and four children!"

If I bent over the fascinating abysses of terror that

opened in many a romance, there swarmed there plenty of classically white ghosts, sorcerers, shadows and malevolent monsters, but the denizens of that world could never climb up my long plaits to get at me, because a few magic words kept them at bay.

"Have you been reading that ghost story, Minet-Chéri? It's a lovely story, isn't it? I can't imagine anything lovelier than the description of the ghost wandering by moonlight in the churchyard. The part, you know, where the author says that the moonlight shone right through the ghost and that it cast no shadow on the grass. A ghost must be a wonderful thing to see. I only wish I could see one; I should call you at once if I did. Unfortunately, they don't exist. But if I could become a ghost after my death, I certainly should, to please you and myself too. And have you read that idiotic story about a dead woman's revenge? I ask you, did you ever hear such rubbish! What would be the use of dying if one didn't gain more sense by it? No, my child, the dead are a peaceful company. I don't fall out with my living neighbours, and I'll undertake to keep on good terms with the dead ones!"

I hardly know what literary coldness, healthy on the whole, protected me from romantic delirium, and caused me—a little later, when I sampled certain books of time-honoured and supposedly infallible seductiveness— to be critical when I should by rights have fallen an intoxicated victim. There again I was perhaps influenced by my mother, whose innate innocence made her inclined to deny evil, even when her curiosity led her to seek it out, and to consider it, jumbled up with good, with wondering eyes.

"This one? Oh, this isn't a harmful book, Minet-Chéri," she would say. "Yes, I know there's one scene, one chapter . . . But it's only a novel. Nowadays writers sometimes run short of ideas, you know. You might have waited a year or two before reading it, perhaps. But after all, Minet-Chéri, you must learn to use your judgment. You've got enough sense to keep it to yourself if you understand too much, and perhaps there are no such things as harmful books."

Nevertheless, there were those that my father locked away in his thuya-wood desk. But chiefly it was the author's name that he locked away.

"I fail to see the use of these children reading Zola!"

Zola bored him, and rather than seek in his pages for reasons that would explain why he allowed or forbade us to read him, he placed upon the index a vast, complete Zola, periodically increased by further yellow deposits.

"Mother, why aren't I allowed to read Zola?"

Her grey eyes, so unskilled at dissimulation, revealed their perplexity.

"It's quite true there are certain Zola's that I would rather you didn't read."

"Then let me have the ones that aren't 'certain'."

She gave me *La Faute de l'Abbé Mouret*, *Le Docteur Pascal* and *Germinal*, but I, wounded at the mistrust that locked away from me a corner of that house where all doors were open, where cats came and went by night and the cellar and larder were mysteriously depleted, was determined to have the others. I got them. Although she may be ashamed of it later, a girl of fourteen has no difficulty, and no credit, in deceiving two trustful parents. I went out into the garden with my first pilfered book. Like several others by Zola it contained a rather insipid story of heredity, in which an amiable and healthy woman gives up her beloved cousin to a sickly friend, and all of it might well have been written by Ohnet, God knows, had the puny wife not known the joy of bringing a child into the world. She produced it suddenly, with a blunt, crude wealth of detail, an anatomical analysis, a dwelling on the colour, odour, contortions and cries, wherein I recognised nothing of my quiet country-bred experience. I felt credulous, terrified, threatened in my dawning feminity. The matings of browsing cattle, of tom cats covering their females like jungle beasts, the simple, almost austere precision of the farmers' wives discussing their virgin heifer or their daughter in labour, I summoned them all to my rescue. But above all I invoked the exorcising voice.

"When you came into the world, my last born, Minet-Chéri, I suffered for three days and two nights. When I was carrying you I was as big as a house. Three days seems a long time. The beasts put us to shame, we women who can no longer bear our children joyfully. But I've never regretted my suffering. They do say that children like you, who have been carried so high in the womb and have taken so long to come down into the daylight, are always the children that are most loved, because they have lain so near their mother's heart and have been so unwilling to leave her."

Vainly I hoped that the gentle words of exorcism, hastily summoned, would sing in my ears, where a metallic reverberation was deafening me. Beneath my eyes other words painted the flesh split open, the excrement, the polluted blood. I managed to raise my head, and saw a bluish garden and smoke-coloured walls wavering strangely under a sky turned yellow. I collapsed on the grass, prostrate and limp like one of those little leverets that the poachers bring, fresh killed, into the kitchen.

When I regained consciousness, the sky was blue once

more, and I lay at the feet of my mother, who was rubbing my nose with eau de Cologne.

"Are you better, Minet-Chéri?"

"Yes. I can't think what came over me."

The grey eyes, gradually reassured, dwelt on mine.

"I think I know what it was. A smart little rap on the knuckles from Above."

I remained pale and troubled and my mother misunderstood:

"There, there now. There's nothing so terrible as all that in the birth of a child, nothing terrible at all. It's much more beautiful in real life. The suffering is so quickly forgotten, you'll see! The proof that all women forget is that it is only men—and what business was it of Zola's, anyway?—who write stories about it."

PROPAGANDA

WHEN I was eight, nine, ten years of age, my father turned his mind to politics. Born to please and do battle, inventive and good at telling anecdotes, I have thought since that he might as easily have succeeded in swaying a House as in charming a woman. But just as his boundless generosity ruined us all, so his childish confidence blinded him. He trusted in the sincerity of his partisans, in the honour of his opponent, in this case Monsieur Merlou. It was Monsieur Pierre Merlou, later an ephemeral Minister, who ousted my father from the general council and from a candidature for the deputation. Blessings upon his deceased Excellency!

A small collectorship in the Yonne could hardly suffice to maintain, in wise quiescence, a captain of the Zouaves, lacking one leg, fiery tempered, and afflicted with philanthropic views. No sooner did the word "politics" assail his ear with its pernicious tinkle, than he began to think:

"I shall conquer the people by educating them; I shall instruct young people and children in the sacred names of natural history, physics and elementary chemistry. I shall go forth brandishing the magic lantern and the microscope, and distributing throughout the village schools those amusing and instructive coloured pictures in which the weevil, magnified twenty times, humiliates a vulture reduced to the proportions of a bee. I shall give popular lectures against alcoholism that will send forth Poyaudin and Forterrat, habitual drunkards though they be, converted and washed clean in the tears of their repentance!"

He suited the action to the word. The shabby victoria and the aged black mare were duly laden, when the time came, with the magic lantern, the painted diagrams, test tubes, bent pipes and other paraphernalia, the future candidate, his crutches and myself. A cold and placid autumn drained the colour from a cloudless sky, the mare slowed to a walk up every hill, and I leaped to the ground to pick blue sloes and coral spindle-berries from the hedges, and to gather white mushrooms with shell-pink linings. As we passed by the denuded woods there was borne to us a fragrance of fresh truffles and crushed leaves.

Then began for me a time of delight. In the villages the schoolroom, vacated an hour earlier, offered its worn benches for the audience; there I found again the black-board, the weights and measures, and the depressing smell of unwashed children. An oil lamp, swinging from a chain, lit up the faces of those who came, suspicious and unsmiling, to hear the comfortable words. The effort of listening furrowed the brows of the martyrs and made their mouths gape. But far removed from them, on the platform, absorbed in important duties, I savoured the arrogance that inflates the child assistant who supplies the conjuror with the plaster eggs, the silk scarf or the blue-bladed daggers of his craft.

A disconcerted torpor followed by timid applause would greet the termination of the "instructive talk". A mayor in sabots would congratulate my father as though he had barely escaped a shameful conviction. On the threshold of the empty hall, children waited to see the departure of "the gentleman who has only one leg". The cold night air would strike my heated face like a damp handkerchief impregnated with the smell of steaming tillage, cowhouses and oak-bark. The harnessed mare, black against the darkness, whinnied at our coming, and turned the horned shadow of her head towards us in the halo of one of the carriage lamps. But my always open-handed father would never leave his melancholy flock without offering a drink to the municipal council at least. At the nearest tavern the hot wine would be steaming on the embers, with the flotsam and jetsam of lemon peel and cinnamon bubbling on its purple swell. The heady vapour, when I think of it, still moistens my nostrils. My father, as a good southerner, would accept nothing but a bottle of lemonade, but his daughter . . .

"The little lady must warm herself with a thimbleful of hot wine!"

A thimbleful? My glass was held out and if the drawer was too hasty in raising the spout of the jug, I knew well how to command, "To the brim!" and how to add, "Your health!" I would clink glasses and lift my elbow, tap on the table with my empty beaker and, using the back of my hand to remove any moustaches of mulled burgundy, I would push my glass a second time towards the jug, remarking: "That warms the cockles!" Oh! I knew how to behave!

My rustic courtesy reassured the drinkers, who would suddenly catch a glimpse in my father of a man much the same as themselves—save for his missing leg—and "well-spoken, if a bit daft". The dreary session would end in laughter, with slaps on the back and tall stories bellowed in voices like those of sheepdogs that sleep out in all seasons,—and I would fall asleep, completely tipsy, my head on the table, lulled by the friendly tumult. Finally, labourers' brawny arms would pick me up and deposit me tenderly at the bottom of the carriage, well swaddled in the red tartan shawl that smelt of orris root and of my mother.

Ten miles, sometimes fifteen, a real expedition under

the breathless stars of a winter sky, to the trot of the mare gorged on oats. Are there really people who remain unmoved and never feel their throats tighten with a childish sob when they hear the sound of a trotting horse upon a frozen road, the bark of a hunting fox or the hoot of an owl struck by the light of the passing carriage-lamps?

On the first few occasions, my return in a condition of beatific prostration rather surprised my mother, who put me quickly to bed, reproaching my father for my evident exhaustion. Then one night she discovered in my glance a hilarity unmistakably burgundian, and in my breath, alas, the secret of my mirth!

Next day the victoria set forth without me and returned that evening, to set forth no more.

"Have you given up your lectures?" enquired my mother of my father a few days later.

He bestowed upon me a sidelong glance of melancholy flattery and shrugged his shoulders:

"Damn it all! You've robbed me of my best election agent!"

FATHER AND MADAME BRUNEAU

NINE o'clock; summer; a garden looking larger in the
evening shadows; rest before sleep. Hurried steps
on the gravel from the terrace to the pump, from the
pump to the kitchen. Sitting close to the ground upon an
uncomfortable little foot-stool, I rest my head, as I do
every evening, against my mother's knees, and guess with
my eyes closed: 'That's Morin's heavy step, on his way
back from watering the tomatoes. That's Mélie emptying
the potato parings. A little high-heeled step: here's
Madame Bruneau come to have a chat with Mother.'

A charming voice reaches me from above:

"Minet-Chéri, what about saying good evening nicely
to Madame Bruneau?"

"She's half asleep, the little darling, let her be."

"Minet-Chéri, if you really are asleep you'd better go to
bed."

"Not just yet, mother, not till a little later! I'm not a
bit sleepy."

A slender hand strokes my hair and pinches my ear.
How dearly I love its three little hard lumps caused by the
rake, the secateur and the dibble.

"Of course not, children of eight are never sleepy."

In the failing light I remain leaning against my mother's
knees. Wide awake, I close my useless eyes. The linen
frock under my cheek smells of household soap, of the
wax that is used to polish the iron, and of violets. If I
move my face a little away from the fragrant gardening
frock, my head plunges into a flood of scents that flows
over us like an unbroken wave: the white tobacco plant
opens to the night its slender scented tubes and its starlike

petals. A ray of light strikes the walnut tree and wakens it; it rustles, stirred to its lowest branches by a slim shaft of moonshine, and the breeze overlays the scent of the white tobacco with the bitter, cool smell of the little worm-eaten walnuts that fall on the grass.

The ray of moonlight reaches down to the flagged terrace and there gives rise to a mellow baritone voice: my father's voice, singing "Page, Squire and Captain." Presently, no doubt, he will change to:

> *I think of thee, I see thee, I adore thee,*
> *At every moment, always, everywhere . . .*

Or perhaps, since Madame Bruneau loves melancholy music, he will give us:

> *Weary of battle, his song arose*
> *From the banks where fatal Dnieper flows.*

But this evening the voice is full of inflexions, agile and awesomely deep, as it broods over scenes of the past.

> *When the fair queen her crown and state forgot*
> *All for the love of her comely page!*

"The Captain's voice would really grace any theatre," sighs Madame Bruneau.

"If he'd only had a mind to . . ." replies my mother proudly. "He is so talented."

The rays of the rising moon fall at last on the angular silhouette of a man standing on the terrace. One hand, so white that it appears green in the moonlight, grips a bar of the railing. His crutch and stick lean against the wall, discarded. My father rests like a heron upon his one leg and sings.

"Ah!" Madame Bruneau sighs again, "every time I hear the captain sing, I feel sad. You can have no idea what it means to lead such a life as mine. To grow old beside a husband like my poor husband. To tell myself that I shall die without ever having known love."

"Madame Bruneau," the stirring voice interrupts her, "you know that my offer still holds good?"

In the shadows I know that Madame Bruneau gives a start and I hear the shifting of her feet on the gravel.

"The wicked man! The wicked man! Captain, you will force me to run away!"

"Sixpence and a packet of tobacco," says the placid, beautiful voice, "because it is you. Sixpence and a packet of tobacco as payment for teaching you the meaning of love; d'you really think it excessive? Don't be stingy, Madame Bruneau! When my prices go up, you'll regret the present terms. Sixpence and a packet of tobacco."

I hear the scandalised exclamations of Madame Bruneau, her hurried flight, the plump, flabby little woman with greying temples, and I hear my mother's words of indulgent reproof, calling my father, as always, by our surname:

"Oh, Colette! Colette!"

My father's voice launches one more romantic couplet at the moon and gradually I cease to hear him, forgetting, as I sleep against the knees so careful of my repose, both Madame Bruneau, and the risky pleasantries that she comes here to seek on fine summer nights.

But next day, and on all the days that follow, our neighbour, Madame Bruneau, no matter how careful a watch she keeps, peering out before dashing across the road as though under a shower, will not escape her enemy, her idol.

Proudly erect upon his solitary leg, or seated and

rolling a cigarette with one hand, or ambushed treacherously behind the unfolded pages of *Le Temps*, he is always there. She may run past, gathering her skirts in both hands as for a country dance, or she may creep noiselessly along by the houses, sheltering under her violet sunshade, but he will challenge her, light-hearted and attractive.

"Sixpence and a packet of tobacco!"

There are souls with an almost endless capacity for hiding their suffering and their trembling responsiveness to the lure of sin. Madame Bruneau was one of these. As long as she could, she bore with my father's scandalous suggestions and cynical glances, pretending to laugh at them. Then, one fine day, deserting her little house, and removing her furniture and her ludicrous husband, she departed to live far away from us, up in the hills, at Bel-Air.

MY MOTHER AND THE ANIMALS

A SUCCESSION of harsh sounds, made by the train, cabs, and omnibuses, is all that my memory retains of a brief visit to Paris when I was six years old. Of a week in Paris five years later I remember nothing but arid heat, panting thirst, feverish fatigue and fleas in a hotel bedroom in the Rue St. Roch.

I remember also that I kept on gazing upwards, vaguely oppressed by the height of the houses, and that a photographer won my heart by calling me, as he doubtless called every child, a 'wonder'.

Five years in the country followed without so much as a thought of Paris.

But when I was sixteen, on returning to Puisaye after a fortnight of theatres, museums and shops, I brought home with me, among memories of finery and greediness, mixed with hopes, regrets, and feelings of scorn, as innocent and awkward as myself, the surprise and the melancholy aversion aroused in me by what I called houses without animals.

Mere cubes without gardens, flowerless abodes where no cat mews behind the dining-room door, where one never treads near the fireside on some part of a dog sprawling like a rug; rooms devoid of familiar spirits, wherein the hand seeking a friendly caress encounters only inanimate wood, or marble, or velvet; I left all these with famished senses, with a vehement need to touch once again fleeces and leaves, warm feathers and the exciting dewiness of flowers.

As if I were discovering them all together again, I

extended my composite greeting to my mother, the garden and the circle of animals.

My return coincided with the watering of the garden, and I still cherish happy memories of the sixth hour of the evening, the green watering-can soaking the blue sateen frock, the strong smell of leaf-mould, and the afterglow that cast a pink reflection on the pages of a forgotten book, the white petals of the tobacco flowers and the white fur of the cat in her basket.

Nonoche the tortoiseshell had had kittens two days earlier, and Bijou her daughter the following evening, and as for Musette, the Havanese bitch, perennial breeder of bastards . . .

"Minet-Chéri, go and see Musette's puppy!"

So I went off to the kitchen where Musette was engaged in feeding an ash-coloured monster, still half blind and nearly as big as herself. Fathered by some local gun-dog, he tugged like a calf at the delicate teats, strawberry-pink against the silver-pale fur, and trampled rhythmically with extended claws a silky belly that would have suffered severely if . . . if my mother had not cut out and sewed for him, from an old pair of white gloves, suède mittens reaching to his elbows. I never saw a ten days' pup look so much like a gendarme.

How many treasures had bloomed in my absence! I ran to the great basket overflowing with indistinguishable cats. That orange ear certainly belonged to Nonoche, but that plume of a black angora tail could only belong to her daughter Bijou, intolerant as a pretty woman. One long slim dry paw, like that of a black rabbit, threatened the heavens; and a tiny kitten spotted like a civet-cat, slumbering replete and prostrate on its back in the middle of this disorder, looked as though it had been assassinated.

I set to work happily to disentangle the mass of nurses

and well-licked nurslings from which arose a pleasant
smell of new-mown hay, fresh milk and well-tended
fur, and I discovered that Bijou, four times a mother in
three years, from whose teats hung a chaplet of newborn
offspring, was herself engaged in noisily sucking, with an
over-large tongue and a purring not unlike the roar of a
log fire, the milk of the aged Nonoche, who lay inert with
comfort, one paw across her eyes. Bending nearer, I
listened to the double purring, treble and bass, that is the
mysterious prerogative of the feline race; a rumbling as of
a distant factory, a whirring as of a captive moth, a frail
mill whose profound slumber stops its grinding. I was
not surprised at the chain of mutually suckling cats.
To those who live in the country and use their eyes
everything becomes alike miraculous and simple. We
had long considered it natural that a bitch should nourish
a kitten, that a cat should select as her lair the top of the
cage wherein trustful green canaries sang happily, their
beaks from time to time plucking from the sleeper an
occasional silky hair for nesting purposes.

A whole year of my childhood was devoted to the task
of capturing, in the kitchen or the cow-house, the rare
flies of winter for the benefit of two swallows, October
nestlings thrown down to us by a gale. Was it not essential
to preserve them and to find provender for their insatiable
beaks that disdained any but living prey?

It was thanks to them that I learned how infinitely a
tame swallow can surpass, in insolent sociability, even
the most pampered of dogs. Our two swallows spent their
time perching on a shoulder or a head, nestling in the
work-basket, running about under the table like chickens,
pecking at the nonplussed dog or chirping in the very

face of the disconcerted cat. They came to school in my pocket and returned home by air. As soon as the shining sickle of their wings grew and sharpened, they would vanish at any time into the vault of the spring sky, but a single shrill call of "Ti-i-inies" would bring them cleaving the wind like two arrows, to alight in my hair, to which they would cling with all the strength of their little curved black steel claws.

All was faery and yet simple among the fauna of my early home. You could never believe that a cat could eat strawberries? And yet, because I have seen him so many times, I know that Babou, that black Satan, interminable and as sinuous as an eel, would carefully select in Madame Pomié's kitchen garden the ripest of the Royal Sovereigns or the Early Scarlets. He it was, too, who would be discovered poetically absorbed in smelling newly-opened violets.

Have you ever heard tell of Pelisson's spider that so passionately loved music? I for one am ready to believe it and also to add, as my slender contribution to the sum of human knowledge, the story of the spider that my mother kept—as my father expressed it—on her ceiling, in that year that ushered in my sixteenth spring. A handsome garden spider she was, her belly like a clove of garlic emblazoned with an ornate cross. In the daytime she slept, or hunted in the web that she had spun across the bedroom ceiling. But during the night, towards three o'clock in the morning, at the moment when her chronic insomnia caused my mother to relight the lamp and open her bedside book, the great spider would also wake, and after a careful survey would lower herself from the ceiling by a thread, directly above the little oil lamp upon which a bowl of chocolate simmered through the night. Slowly she would descend, swinging limply to and fro like a big bead, and grasping the edge of the cup with all her eight legs, she would bend over head foremost and drink to satiety. Then she would draw herself ceiling-wards again, heavy with creamy chocolate, her ascent punctuated by the pauses and meditations imposed by an overloaded stomach, and would resume her post in the centre of her silken rigging.

Still wearing my travelling coat, I sat dreaming, weary, enchanted and re-enslaved in the midst of my kingdom.

"Where is your spider, mother?"

My mother's grey eyes, magnified by her glasses, clouded:

"Have you come back from Paris only to ask for news of the spider, you ungrateful child?"

I hung my head, awkward in my affection, ashamed of that which was best in me:

"I couldn't help remembering sometimes, at night, at the spider's hour, when I couldn't sleep. . . ."

"Minet-Chéri, you couldn't sleep? Was your bed un-comfortable? The spider's in her web, I suppose. But do come and see if my caterpillar is hibernating. I really think she's going to become a chrysalis, and I've given her a little box of dry sand. She's an Emperor moth caterpillar and I think a bird must have pecked her stomach but she's quite well again now."

The caterpillar was perhaps asleep, moulded to the form of a supporting twig of box thorn. The ravages around her testified to her vitality. There were nothing but shreds of leaves, gnawed stems and barren shoots. Plump, as thick as my thumb and over four inches long, she swelled the fat rolls of her cabbage-green body, adorned at intervals with hairy warts of turquoise blue. I detached her gently from her twig and she writhed in anger, exposing her paler stomach and all her spiky little paws that clung leechlike to the branch to which I returned her.

"But, mother, she has devoured everything!"

The grey eyes behind the spectacles wavered perplexedly from the denuded twigs to the caterpillar and thence to my face:

"But what can I do about it? And after all, the box thorn she's eating, you know, is the one that strangles honeysuckle."

"Yes, but won't the caterpillar eat the honeysuckle too?"

"I don't know. But in any case, what can I do about it? I can hardly kill the creature."

The scene is before me as I write, the garden with its sun-warmed walls, the last of the black cherries hanging on the tree, the sky webbed with long pink clouds. I can feel again beneath my fingers the vigorous resentment of the caterpillar, the wet, leathery hydrangea leaves, and my mother's little work-worn hand.

I can evoke the wind at will and make it rustle the stiff papery blades of the bamboos and sing, through the comb-like leaves of the yew, as a worthy accompaniment to the voice that on that day and on all the other days, even to the final silence, spoke words that had always the same meaning.

"That child must have proper care. Can't we save that woman? Have those people got enough to eat? I can hardly kill the creature."

EPITAPHS

" AND what did he do when he was alive, this Astoniphronque Bonscop of yours?"

My brother threw back his head, clasped his hands
round his knee and narrowed his eyes as he sought to
distinguish, at a distance inaccessible to imperfect human
vision, the forgotten features of Astoniphronque
Bonscop.

"He was a town-crier. But at home he repaired cane-
bottomed chairs. He was a burly chap . . . er . . . not very
interesting. He drank and used to beat his wife."

"Then why have you put 'a good husband and a good
father' on his epitaph?"

"Because that's what you always put when people are
married."

"Who else has died since yesterday?"

"Madame Egrémimy Pulitien."

"What was she, Madame Egrélimy? . . ."

"Egrémimy, with a 'y' at the end. Just a lady who was
always dressed in black. She wore cotton gloves——"

My brother broke off and whistled between his teeth,
which were set on edge by the mere thought of cotton
gloves rubbing against finger-nails.

He was thirteen and I was seven. With his close-
cropped black hair and his light blue eyes he looked like a
young Italian model. He was as gentle as could be, and
utterly unmanageable.

"By the way," he went on, "be ready to-morrow at ten
o'clock. There's a service."

"What service?"

"A service for the repose of the soul of Lugustu Trutrumèque."

"The father or the son?"

"The father."

"I can't manage ten o'clock. I shall be at school."

"So much the worse for you; you won't see the service. Now let me alone, I must think out an epitaph for Madame Egrémimy Pulitien."

In spite of this warning, which savoured of a command, I followed my brother up to the loft, where, upon a trestle table, he cut and glued sheets of white cardboard into the shapes of upright or flat tombstones, or of square mausoleums surmounted by a cross. These he subsequently decorated in ornamental capitals of indian ink, with short or lengthy epitaphs, perpetuating in the purest "monumental mason" style, the sorrow of the surviving and the virtues of the supposed deceased.

"*Here lies Astoniphronque Bonscop, who departed this life 22 June, 1874, aged fifty-seven. A good husband and a good father, heaven awaits him and the earth deplores his loss. Passer-by, give him your prayers!*"

These few lines stood out in dark letters upon an elegant little tombstone shaped like a romanesque door, with the mouldings executed in watercolour. A strut, similar to those used in the manufacture of standard photograph frames, supported it at a gracefully inclined angle.

"It's a bit bald," remarked my brother, "but for a town crier . . . I'll make up for it with Madame Egrémimy." And he unbent so far as to read me an experimental draft.

" '*O thou model of Christian spouses! Reft from us at the age of eighteen, already four times a mother! The lamentations*

*of thy weeping children have not availed to keep thee with them!
Thy business is in jeopardy and thy husband vainly seeks oblivion!'* That's as far as I've got."

"It's a good beginning. And she had four children
before she was eighteen?"

"Haven't I told you so?"

"And what about her business being in jeopardy? What
is a business in jeopardy?"

My brother shrugged his shoulders.

"You couldn't possibly understand that, a girl of
seven. Put the glue-pot into the double saucepan, and
prepare me two small wreaths of blue beads for the
Azioume twins' mausoleum. They were born and died on
the same day."

"Oh! . . . Were they nice?"

"Very nice," said my brother. "Two boys, both fair
and exactly alike. I've thought out a new scheme for their
grave. Two broken columns of rolled cardboard painted
to imitate marble and each column surrounded by a
wreath of beads. You wait and see, old girl!"

He whistled in admiration and then worked on in
silence. All around him the loft blossomed with small
white tombs, a cemetery for big dolls. His mania involved
no irreverent parody, no morbid display. He had never
knotted the strings of an apron under his chin to simulate a
chasuble or intoned the *Dies Irae*. But he loved cemeteries
as other people rejoice in formal gardens, ornamental
water, or kitchen-gardens. He would set forth on winged
feet to visit the village churchyards for ten or fifteen
miles around, and would tell me afterwards of his ex-
plorations.

"At Escamps, old girl, it's really stylish. There's a
notary buried in a chapel as big as a gardener's tool-shed,
and you can look through glass doors and see an altar

and flowers and a hassock on the floor and an upholstered chair."

"A chair! Who for?"

"For the deceased, I suppose, when he comes back at night."

He had retained from his earliest childhood the quiet, self-possessed, aloof attitude to life that protects the very young child from fear of death or of blood. At thirteen he seemed scarcely to distinguish between the dead and the living. While my games evoked before my eyes imaginary persons, transparent and visible, whom I greeted and of whom I asked news of their relations, my brother, inventing his imaginary dead, treated them with the utmost friendliness and adorned them to the best of his ability. He would surmount one with an ornate cross, another he would lay beneath a gothic arch and yet a third would rest peacefully covered only by the epitaph that extolled his earthly life.

A day came when the rough floor of the loft ceased to give satisfaction. My brother desired to honour his white tombs with soft, rich-smelling earth, real grass, cypresses and ivy. At the far end of the garden, behind the grove of thuyas, he established his dead with their resounding names, whose numbers overflowed the lawn planted with marigold heads and little bead wreaths. The diligent sexton surveyed them with the eye of an artist.

"How well they look!"

A week later my mother passed that way, paused in amazement, and stared with all her eyes—her lorgnette, her pince-nez and finally her long-distance glasses—and exclaimed in horror, stamping right and left among the graves.

"That child will end his days in a criminal cell! This

is delirium, sadism, vampirism, sacrilege, it is . . . I really don't know what it is!"

Across the abyss that separates a child from a grown-up person, she gazed at the culprit and with an angry rake swept away tombstones, wreaths and mutilated memorial columns. My brother endured without protest the holding up of his work to obloquy. Left in contemplation of the empty lawn, and of the freshly raked earth shaded by the hedge of thuyas, he called me to witness, with a poet's melancholy:

"Don't you think it looks sad, a garden without graves?"

"MY FATHER'S DAUGHTER"

WHEN I was between fourteen and fifteen years old, with long arms, straight back, too small a chin and clear blue eyes that lifted at the corners when I smiled, my mother took to staring at me with an odd expression on her face. She would sometimes allow her book or her needlework to rest on her knees while from over her glasses she bent on me a grey-blue glance of surprise, almost of suspicion.

"What have I done this time, mother?"

"It's only that . . . you're getting to look like my father's daughter."

Then she would frown and take up her book or her needle again. One day she added to the above reply, which had become traditional, a further comment:

"You know who I mean by my father's daughter?"

"Why, yourself, of course!"

"No, young woman, not myself."

"Oh! Then you're not your father's daughter?"

She laughed, in no wise scandalised by a liberty of speech which she habitually encouraged:

"Good heavens, yes! Of course I am, like all the others. And the Lord only knows how many he had in all. Half of them I never knew. Irma, Eugène, Paul and myself, were all by the same mother, whom I scarcely remember. But you remind me of my father's daughter, the daughter that he brought us one day as a new-born baby, without even troubling to tell us where she came from, would you believe it! He was known as the Gorilla. You can see how ugly he was, can't you, Minet-Chéri? And yet the women absolutely hung on him."

She pointed with her thimble to a daguerreotype which hung on the wall, a daguerreotype which I now keep in a drawer, and which reveals, under its film of silver, the head and shoulders of a "coloured man"—a quadroon, I believe—wearing a high white cravat, with pale, contemptuous eyes, and a long nose above the thick Negro lips that had inspired his nickname.

"Ugly, but well built," continued my mother. "And attractive too, I can assure you, in spite of his purple fingernails. I've nothing against him except that he gave me his awful mouth."

Hers was a large mouth, true enough, but kind and rosy. I protested:

"He didn't! You know you're pretty."

"I know what I'm saying, and in any case that mouth has gone no further. . . . I was eight years old when my father's daughter came to us. The Gorilla said to me: 'Bring her up. She's your sister.' At eight years old I felt no misgivings, for I knew nothing about babies. Luckily, a wet-nurse arrived with my father's daughter. All the same I found time, while I held her in my arms, to notice that her fingertips were not sufficiently tapered. My father was such an admirer of beautiful hands. Then and there I proceeded, with the cruelty of childhood, to remodel those tender little fingers that seemed to melt between my own. My father's daughter started out in life with ten little round abscesses, five on each hand, at the tips of her well-shaped little fingernails. Now you realize what a wicked mother you've got. Such a lovely new-born baby. How she screamed! The doctor said: "I cannot understand the cause of this digital inflammation." I listened in horror to that word 'digital' and trembled. But I never owned up. Deceit is so strong in children. They generally outgrow it. Do you think you are getting a little less untruthful as you get older, Minet-Chéri?"

It was the first time that my mother had ever accused me of chronic untruthfulness. Everything that an adolescent girl harbours of perverse or delicate dissimulation flinched in me beneath the gaze of those deeply divining and completely undeceived grey eyes. But already she was gently withdrawing the hand that she had placed on my forehead, already the grey eyes, resuming their kindness, their discretion, were generously averted from mine.

"I took good care of her afterwards, you know, of my father's daughter. I learned how to. She grew up pretty, tall, fairer than you are, and you're like her, so like her. I think she married quite young. I'm not certain, though. And that's all I know of her, for my father carried her off, later, just as he had brought her, without condescending to give any reasons. She spent only her early years with us, with Eugène, Paul, Irma and me, and with the big monkey, Jean, in the house where my father manufactured chocolate. In those days chocolate was made with cocoa, sugar and vanilla. At the top of the house the soft bricks of chocolate were put to dry on the terrace. And every morning they showed, printed on them like flowers with five hollow petals, the trails of the nocturnal cats. I used to miss her, my father's daughter, and, would you believe it, Minet-Chéri . . ."

The sequel of her narrative is missing from my memory. The blank is as complete as though I had at that moment been smitten with deafness. The fact was that, indifferent to "My-Father's-Daughter", I left my mother to draw forth from oblivion her beloved dead, while I remained dreaming of a scent and a picture that she had evoked: the smell of the soft bricks of chocolate, and the hollow flowers that bloomed beneath the paws of the vagrant cat.

THE WEDDING

Henriette Boisson will not get married, and I may as well give up expecting it. She carries before her a little round belly seven months gone, which does not prevent her scrubbing the kitchen tiles, or hanging up the washing on the clothes-lines or on the spindle-wood hedge. A belly like that is certainly not an aid to marriage in my part of the country. Madame Pomié and Madame Léger have said to my mother twenty times: "I can't understand you, with a big girl like your daughter, keeping a servant who . . . a servant that . . ."

But my mother has roundly replied that she would rather scandalise the neighbours than turn out an expectant mother and her child.

So there it is, Henriette Boisson will not get married. But Adrienne Septmance, our housemaid, is pretty and lively, and for a month past has been much addicted to song. She sings at her sewing, and adorns her neck with a bow of satin trimmed with lace surrounding a locket in which lead apes marcasite. She thrusts a pearl-edged comb into her black hair and pulls down the folds of her blouse over her inflexible stays every time she passes a looking-glass. These are symptoms familiar to my experience. I am thirteen and a half and I know what it means when a housemaid has an admirer. But will Adrienne Septmance get married? That is the question.

At the Septmances there are four daughters, three sons and some cousins, the entire lot sheltering under an ancient creeper-covered thatch beside the road.

How I shall enjoy a wedding there! For a whole week

my mother will bewail it, will harp on my "low acquaintances" and my "bad ways"; she will threaten to accompany me and will finally give up the idea out of weariness and innate shyness.

I keep an eye on Adrienne Septmance. She sings, hustles through her work, runs in the street, and laughs aloud in an affected manner.

She exudes the common scent that is bought here from Maumond, the hairdresser, a scent that seems to catch in one's tonsils and that suggests the sweetish smell of horse's urine drying on a road.

"Adrienne, you smell of patchouli!" declares my mother, who never knew what patchouli was.

Finally, in the kitchen, I come across a youth whose face looks dusky under his white straw hat, and who sits against the wall in the complete silence that pertains to the honourable suitor. I am filled with triumph and my mother with gloom.

"Who shall we get after she goes?" she enquires of my father at dinner.

But had my father even noticed that Adrienne Septmance had succeeded Marie Bardin?

"They've invited us," adds my mother. "Of course, I shan't go. But Adrienne has asked me to allow the little one to be bridesmaid. It's really very awkward."

The "little one" springs to her feet and spins her prepared yarn.

"Mother, I can go with Julie David and all the Follet girls. You know quite well that with all the Follets there you needn't worry, it'll be just the same as if you were going yourself; and Madame Follet's cart is to take us and bring us back and she has said that her girls aren't to dance later than ten o'clock, and . . ."

I grow red and fall silent for, instead of protesting,

my mother envelops me in a glance full of scorn and mockery.

"I was thirteen and a half once," she remarks. "You needn't exhaust yourself any further. Why not say quite simply: 'I adore servants' weddings'?"

My white frock with the purple sash, my hair hanging loose and making me hot, my bronze shoes—far too small, alas!—and my white stockings, everything has been ready since the evening before. In fact my hair, plaited to give it a wave, has been torturing my temples for forty-eight hours.

It is a fine day, indeed scorching, just the weather for pastoral weddings. The Mass has not been unduly long. In the procession the Follet boy has offered me his arm, but once the procession is over, what should he do with a partner of thirteen years? . . . Madame Follet drives the cart that overflows with us and our laughter, with her four daughters dressed alike in blue, with Julie David in shot pink and mauve alpaca. The carts rattle along the road and we are coming to the moment that I like best of all.

Where did I get my violent passion for rustic wedding-breakfasts? What ancestor bequeathed to me, via my frugal parents, a positively religious fervour for stewed rabbit, leg of mutton with garlic, soft-boiled eggs in red wine, all served between barn walls draped with buff sheets decorated with branches of red June roses? I am only thirteen, and the familiar menu of these four-o'clock repasts does not appal me. Glass basins filled with loaf sugar are strewn about the table: everyone knows that they are so placed in order that the guests, between courses, may suck lumps of sugar soaked in wine, an infallible method of loosening the tongue and of renewing the appetite. Bouilloux and Labbé, gargantuan freaks, indulge in a guzzling match here as at all weddings. Labbé drinks white wine from a pail used for milking the cows, and Bouilloux is offered an entire leg of mutton, which he consumes unaided, leaving nothing but the bare bone.

What with songs, feasting and carousing, Adrienne's wedding is a lovely wedding. Five meat courses, three sweets and the tiered wedding-cake surmounted by a trembling plaster rose. Since four o'clock the open doorway of the barn has framed the green pond shaded by elms, and a patch of sky now gradually flushing with the evening glow. Adrienne Septmance, dark, and unfamiliar in her cloud of tulle, leans languorously against her husband's shoulder and wipes the sweat from a shining face. A tall, bony peasant bellows patriotic songs, "Paris must be saved! Paris must be saved!" and he encounters looks of awe, because his voice is powerful and sad, and he himself comes from so great a distance: "Just think! A man from Dampierre-sous-Bouhy! At least thirty miles from here!" The swallows dart and scream above the drinking cattle. The bride's mother is weeping for no particular reason. Julie David has stained her dress; the dresses of the four Follet girls are as blue as phosphorus in the gathering gloom. The candles will not be lighted until the ball begins. A happiness in advance of any years, a subtle happiness of satiated greed, keeps me sitting there peacefully gorged with rabbit stew, boiled chicken and sweetened wine.

The shrill sound of Rouillard's violin suddenly stirs the stumps of all the Follets, of Julie and the bride and the young farmers' wives in their goffered bonnets. "Take your places for the quadrille!" The benches and trestles, together with the now useless Labbé and Bouilloux, are dragged outside. The long June twilight intensifies the smell of manure from the neighbouring rabbit hutch and pigsty. I have no desires, too full to dance, squeamish and superior like one who has thoroughly overeaten. I think the revelry—so far as I am concerned—is over.

"Come for a walk," says Julie David.

She drags me off to the kitchen garden of the farm. The scent of crushed sorrel, sage, and green leeks fills the air as we walk, and my companion chatters. Her hair has lost its woolly curl, achieved by so many curling pins, and her fair skin shines on her cheeks like a polished apple.

"That young Caillon kissed me. . . . And I overheard everything the bridegroom was saying to the bride just now. . . . He said 'One more schottische and we can clear them all out. . . .' Armandine Follet was sick in front of everyone."

I feel hot. Her moist childish arm is pressed against mine, which I remove. I don't like other people's skins. At the back of the farmhouse one window is open and lighted up; the moths and mosquitoes are clustering round a smoking oil lamp.

"That's the bedroom for the married couple!" whispers Julie.

The bedroom for the married couple! A huge wardrobe of black pear-wood dwarfs the low-pitched whitewashed room, and a straw-bottomed chair is squeezed in between it and the bed. Two very large tightly-packed bunches of roses and camomile are drooping in blue glass vases on the mantelpiece, sending out, even as far as the garden, the strong, faded odour that follows upon a funeral. And there is the high narrow bed beneath its curtains of Turkey red cotton, stuffed with feathers, loaded with down

pillows, the bed that is to stage the final scene of a day
redolent of sweat, incense, the breath of kine and the
aroma of sauces.

A moth singes its wing in the flame of the lamp and
almost puts it out. Leaning on the low window-sill, I
inhale the smell of humanity, thickened by the heavier
smells of dead flowers and paraffin, that is an offence to
the garden. Presently the newly married couple will
come here. I had not thought of that. They will sink into
that mound of feathers. The heavy shutters will be closed
upon them, and the door and all the exits of this stifling
little tomb. Between them will be enacted that obscure
encounter of which my mother's outspoken simplicity
and the lives of the beasts around me have taught me too
much and too little. And afterwards? I am frightened of
the room, of the bed that I had never thought of. My
companion laughs and chatters.

"I say, did you see that the Follet boy was wearing the
rose I gave him in his buttonhole? I say, did you notice
that Nana Bouilloux has put her hair up? And she's only
thirteen! When *I* marry, I shall make no bones about
telling my mother what I . . . But where are you going?
Where are you off to?"

I have fled, trampling on the lettuces, and the raised
ridges of the asparagus bed.

"Wait for me! What on earth's the matter with you?"

Julie does not catch me up until I reach the gate of the
kitchen garden and the red halo of dust surrounding the
lights of the dance floor. There, close to the reassuring
barn that resounds with the tumult of the blaring trom-
bone, of laughter and stamping feet, her impatience
finally extorts the most unexpected of answers, bleated
amid floods of tears by a bewildered little girl:

"I want to go home to mother."

MY SISTER WITH THE LONG HAIR

I WAS twelve years old, with the manners and vocabulary of an intelligent, rather uncouth boy, but my gait was not boyish because my figure already showed signs of development, and above all because I wore my hair in two long plaits that swished through the air around me like whips. These I used indiscriminately as ropes from which to hang the picnic basket, as brushes to be dipped in ink or in paint, as whips for a recalcitrant dog or as ribbons to make the cat play. My mother wailed to see me maltreat these two golden brown thongs for whose sake I was daily condemned to get up half an hour earlier than my school-fellows. At seven o'clock on dark winter mornings I would fall asleep again, sitting before the wood fire, while my mother brushed and combed my nodding head. From those mornings I date my invincible hatred of long hair. Long hairs would be discovered tangled in the lower branches of the trees in the garden, long hairs attached to the cross-beam from which hung the trapeze and the swing. A pullet in the barnyard was supposed to be lame from birth, until we ascertained that a long hair, covered with pimply skin was bound tightly round one of its feet and atrophying it.

Long hair, barbaric adornment, fleece to which clings an animal smell, hair that one cherishes in secret for secret purposes, that one displays when twisted or plaited and conceals when it is dishevelled; who bathes in your torrent rippling to the waist? A woman surprised when she is doing her hair, flies as though she were naked. Amorous dalliance sees no more of you than the passerby.

Unbound, you fill the bed with a mesh that irritates a sensitive epidermis, trailing weeds that confuse a wandering hand. There is just one moment, in the evening, when the pins are withdrawn and the shy face shines out for an instant from between the tangled waves; and there is a similar moment in the early morning. And because of those two moments everything that I have just written against long hair counts for nothing at all.

With my hair plaited Alsatian fashion, two little bows swinging at the ends of my two plaits and a parting down the middle of my head, disfigured by my uncovered temples and by ears too distant from my nose, I would sometimes climb the stairs to visit my sister with the long hair. At noon she would already be reading, as luncheon finished at eleven o'clock. In bed, in the mornings, she would still be reading. The sound of the opening door would hardly win a glance from her absent, slanting black eyes, blurred with some tender romance or bloodthirsty adventure. A candle stump bore witness to her night-long vigil. The wallpaper, pearl-grey with a design of cornflowers, showed traces, near the bed, of the many matches that my long-haired sister, with a rough and heedless hand, had struck on its surface. Her chaste nightgown, with its long sleeves and small turned-down collar, revealed only her strange little head, attractive in its ugliness with the high cheek-bones and the sarcastic mouth of a pretty Kalmuck girl. The thick mobile eyebrows were constantly on the move like silky caterpillars and her low forehead, her ears and the nape of her neck, all of her that was faintly anæmic white flesh, seemed foredoomed to be overrun by her hair.

Juliette's hair was so abnormal in length, vigour and

thickness, that I never knew it to arouse, as it might well have done, either jealousy or admiration. My mother spoke of it as of an incurable misfortune. "Oh, dear!" she would murmur with a heavy sigh, "I must go and brush Juliette's hair." On holidays I would see her at ten o'clock coming down exhausted from the upper floor. She would throw down the paraphernalia of brushes and combs, exclaiming: "I'm completely worn out. My left leg hurts me. I've just finished brushing Juliette's hair."

Black, with threads of auburn, and falling in heavy waves, Juliette's hair, when it was loose, exactly covered her from top to toe. As my mother undid the plaits a dark curtain descended, progressively concealing the girl's back, her shoulders, her face and her skirt until one beheld only a curious conical tent, made of dark silk with great parallel waves, revealing for an instant an asiatic countenance, and stirred at moments by two little hands that fumbled amid the curtains of the tent.

The shelter would be twisted into four plaits, four cables as thick as a stout wrist and shining like water snakes. Two of them started from the temples, two others from the nape of the neck on either side of a parting of bluish skin. A kind of absurd diadem was then erected above the young forehead and another bun of plaits loaded the drooping neck. Yellowed photographs of Juliette attest the fact; never was a young girl's hair more hideously dressed.

"Poor little wretch!" Madame Pomié would exclaim, clasping her hands. "Can't you put your hat on straight?" Madame Donnot would ask Juliette, on coming out from Mass. "Of course I know that with your hair. . . . Life can hardly be worth living, I should say, with hair like yours."

On Thursday mornings, then, towards ten o'clock, I would often find my long-haired sister still abed and reading. Always pale and absorbed, she read in a grim kind of way, with a cup of chocolate grown cold beside her. She took no more heed of my arrival than of the cries of, "Get up, Juliette!" coming from below stairs. She would read on, mechanically twining one of her snake-like plaits round her wrist and sometimes turning towards me an unseeing glance, that sexless, ageless glance of the obsessed, full of obscure defiance and an incomprehensible irony.

In that young girl's bedroom I enjoyed a lofty boredom of which I was very proud. The rosewood bureau was crammed with inaccessible wonders; my long-haired sister was no novice with pastels, the box of compasses, and a certain crescent of transparent white horn engraved with centimetres and millimetres, the memory of which sometimes makes my mouth water as a cut lemon does. Then there was greasy dark-blue transfer-paper for embroidery and a pricker for piercing the holes in "broderie anglaise", shuttles for tatting made of almond-white ivory, bobbins of peacock-coloured silk, and a Chinese bird painted on rice-paper that my sister was copying in satin-stitch on a velvet panel. There were ball programmes too, with mother-of-pearl leaves, attached to the useless fan of a young girl who never went to balls.

Having overcome my covetousness, I would grow bored, although from the window I could look straight into the garden opposite where our cat Zoë was chastising an unknown tom. And, moreover, in Madame Saint-Alban's garden, next door, the rare clematis—the one that displays, under the fleshy white texture of its flowers, fine mauve veins like thin blood flowing beneath a delicate skin—fell in a luminous cascade of six-pointed stars.

Then, again, to my left, at the corner of the narrow Rue des Sœurs, Tatave, the lunatic who was said to be harmless, emitted a hideous din without moving a feature of his face. None the less, I was bored.

"Juliette, what are you reading? Do tell me what you're reading, Juliette?"

The answer was infinitely slow to come, as though leagues of space and silence lay between us.

"*Froment jeune et Risler aîné.*" Or else, "*La Chartreuse de Parme.*"

La Chartreuse de Parme, Le Vicomte de Bragelonne, Monsieur de Camors, Le Vicaire de Wakefield, La Chronique de Charles IX, La Terre, Lorenzaccio, Les Monstres parisiens, Grande Maguet, Les Misérables. Poetry too, but less often. Serials from *Le Temps,* cut out and sewn together; the collection of the *Revue des Deux Mondes,* and those of the *Revue Bleue* and of the *Journal des Dames et des Demoiselles,* Voltaire and Ponson du Terrail. Novels were stuffed among the cushions, wedged into the work-basket, or languished forgotten in the garden, soaked by the rain. My long-haired sister no longer spoke, ate scarcely anything, seemed surprised to meet us about the house, and woke with a start if a bell rang.

My mother lost her temper, sat up of nights to put out the lamp and confiscate candles; my long-haired sister caught a cold, demanded a night-light in order to prepare hot infusions and read by the night-light's glimmer. After the night-light, there were boxes of matches and the moonlight. After the moonlight, my long-haired sister, exhausted by romantic insomnia, became feverish, and her fever refused to yield either to compresses or purgative draughts.

"It's typhoid," announced Doctor Pomié one morning.

"Typhoid? Oh, come now, Doctor, why? You can't really mean it?"

My mother was vaguely shocked and astonished, not anxious as yet. I remember her standing on the steps, gaily waving the doctor's prescription, like a handkerchief.

"Goodbye, Doctor! Come again soon! Yes, to-morrow, that's right, come again to-morrow!"

Plump and active, she bustled up and down the steps, scolding the dog who did not want to go back home. Still holding the prescription, with an incredulous grimace, she went back to my sister whom we had left asleep, muttering feverishly. Juliette was now awake, her four plaits and her black, Mongol eyes gleaming darkly against the white bed.

"You can't get up to-day, my darling," said my mother. "Doctor Pomié won't hear of it. Would you like some nice cold lemonade? Shall I straighten your bed?"

My long-haired sister did not answer at once. But her oblique eyes were fixed upon us with an alert look wherein flickered an unfamiliar smile, a smile that sought to please. After a moment's silence:

"Is that you, Catulle?" she enquired in a light voice.

My mother hesitated and then stepped forward.

"Catulle? Who is Catulle?"

"Why, Catulle Mendès, of course," the light voice replied. "Is that you? I've come, you see. I've put your fair hair in the oval locket. Octave Feuillet was here this morning, but what a difference! From his photograph alone, I had decided . . . I can't endure whiskers. And in any case I only like fair men. Did I tell you that I'd put a touch of red pastel on your photograph, on the mouth? That was because of your verses. It must be that touch of red that has given me such a headache since then. No, we shan't meet anyone . . . For that matter, I don't know anyone in these parts. It's all because of that little touch of red . . . and because of the kiss. Catulle . . . I don't know a soul here. I'm ready to swear before everyone that you, Catulle, are the one and only . . ."

My sister broke off, began to grumble in a harsh, intolerant tone, turned her face to the wall and continued to complain in a much fainter voice, that seemed to come from a great distance. One of her plaits lay across her face, shining, thick and richly alive. My mother, struck motionless, her head bent as though in the effort to hear better, stood staring in a kind of horror at this stranger, who in her delirium called only for unknown persons. Then she looked round, caught sight of me and hastily commanded:

"Go away, go downstairs at once."

And as though overcome with shame, she buried her face in her hands.

MATERNITY

No sooner was she married, than my long-haired sister yielded to the persuasions of her husband and her in-laws and stopped seeing us, while the formidable machinery of lawyers and notaries was set in motion. I was only eleven or twelve years old, and I had no idea of the meaning of such expressions as "improvident guardianship", and "inexcusable extravagance", directed against my father. There followed a complete rupture between my parents and the young married couple. To my brothers and myself it made little difference. Whether my half-sister—the tall gracefully-built girl with the Mongolian features, whose amazing hair weighed her down as with chains—shut herself all day in her room upstairs or exiled herself with a husband in a neighbouring house, it came to much the same thing, and did not affect us. In any case, my brothers, who had themselves left home, perceived only the distant reverberations of an upheaval that engrossed our entire village. A domestic tragedy in a great city can run its course discreetly, and its heroes can slaughter each other in silence. But a village that vegetates all the year round in peace and inanition and has to content itself with meagre scandals afforded by local incidents of poaching or gallantry, such a village is without compassion, and its inmates are not likely to avert their eyes in charitable consideration from the spectacle of a woman whom financial disputes have robbed of her child in less than a day.

We were the only topic of conversation. Every morning there was a queue at Léonore's, the butcher's, in the hope that my mother might be cornered and forced to betray some emotion. Creatures who the day before had not appeared bloodthirsty, now gloated together over a few precious tears, a few words of complaint wrested from her maternal indignation. She would come home exhausted, panting like a hunted beast. At home with my father and me, she would pull herself together, cutting up bread for the fowls, basting the roast, hammering away, with all the strength of her small hands and beautiful arms, at a box for the cat who was near her time, or washing my hair with rum and yolk of egg. She made a sort of cruel art of suppressing her grief and sometimes I would even hear her singing. But at evening she would go upstairs to close the shutters of the first floor windows herself, so as to gaze across the party wall at the garden and house where my sister lived. She could see the strawberry beds, the espaliered apple-trees, clumps of phlox and three steps that led up to a terrace with orange trees in tubs and cane chairs. One night—I was standing behind her—we recognised, lying on one of the chairs, a gold and purple shawl which dated from my long-haired sister's latest convalescence. I cried out: "Oh, look! There's Juliette's shawl!" and received no answer. A curious, convulsive sound not unlike stifled laughter died away with my mother's footsteps down the corridor, after she had fastened all the shutters.

Months went by and nothing was altered. The ungrateful daughter remained under her own roof, and passed our threshold without turning her head. But sometimes, meeting my mother unexpectedly, she fled like a child that fears a blow. As for me I would meet her without emotion, only mildly surprised at the sight of this stranger who wore new dresses and unfamiliar hats.

One day the rumour reached us that she was going to

have a child. But I had ceased to think about her, nor did I attach any special significance to the fact that just at that time my mother began to have attacks of nervous faintness, nausea and palpitations. I only remember that the sight of my sister, distorted and grown heavy, filled me with still more embarrassment and disgust.

Still more weeks passed. My mother, always lively and active, began to employ her energies in a rather incoherent manner. One day she seasoned the strawberry tart with salt instead of sugar, and instead of showing distress she met my father's expostulations with a face of stony irony that upset me terribly.

One summer evening, just as we three had finished dinner, a neighbour came in bareheaded, wished us good evening with an important air, whispered a few mysterious words in my mother's ear and departed forthwith. My mother sighed, "Oh my goodness! . . ." and remained standing, her hands resting on the table.

"What's the matter?" enquired my father.

With an effort, she withdrew her gaze from the flame of the lamp and answered:

"Things have started . . . over there. . . ."

I vaguely understood, and went upstairs earlier than usual to my bedroom, one of three that overlooked the garden opposite. After putting out my lamp I opened the window in order to watch, at the end of a garden turned purple under the moonlight, the mysterious house with all its shutters closed. I listened, pressing my beating heart against the window-sill. The scene was bathed in the nocturnal silence of the village, and all I could hear was the bark of a dog and the scraping of a cat's claws on the bole of a tree. Then a shadowy form in a white dressing gown—my mother—crossed the road and entered the garden opposite. I saw her raise her head and consider the party wall as though she had hopes of climbing it. Then she started to walk up and down the centre path, where she broke off a sprig of scented bay, automatically crushing its leaves between her fingers. Under the cold light of the full moon not one of her gestures escaped me. Motionless, her face upturned to the sky, she listened, and waited. A thin cry, long-drawn-out and muffled by distance and the intervening walls, reached us at the same moment, and she clasped her hands convulsively to her breast. A second cry, pitched on the same note, almost like the opening of a melody, floated towards us, and a third. . . . Then I saw my mother grip her own loins with desperate hands, spin round and stamp on the ground as she began to assist and share, by her low groans, by the rocking of her tormented body, by the clasping of her unwanted arms, and by all her maternal anguish and strength, the anguish and strength of the ungrateful daughter who, so near to her and yet so far away, was bringing a child into the world.

"THE RAGE OF PARIS"

"*O*NE *shilling the front rows, sixpence the others, children or standing room threepence.*" Such in those days was the tariff of our artistic entertainments whenever a troupe of strolling players halted for a night at my native village. The town crier, whose duty it was to inform the thirteen hundred inhabitants of the neighbouring county town, announced the event during the morning, towards ten o'clock, to the accompaniment of a drum. The news spread like wildfire. Children like myself shouted shrilly and jumped with joy. Young girls, their heads bristling with curling pins, stood for a moment struck dumb by happy surprise, then flew as if caught in a downpour. And my mother grumbled, but without real conviction: "Good Heavens! Minet-Chéri, you aren't going to drag me to *A Woman's Martyrdom?* I shall be a martyr if you do—it's so unutterably boring." Nevertheless, she would get out the goffering and pleating irons and set about preparing her best lawn tucker.

Smoking lamps with tin reflectors, benches harder than those at school, canvas scenery with the paint flaking off, actors as melancholy as performing animals, what an ennobling sadness you lent to my evening's enjoyment! For the dramas filled me with a cold dismay, and even as a small child I was never able to laugh wholeheartedly at tattered vaudeville or echo the mirth of half-starved funny men.

What can have been the chance that brought us on one occasion a proper troupe of itinerant players, a troupe possessed of good scenery and costumes, all of them well

clad and adequately nourished, under the control of a
sort of manager in riding boots and a dicky of white
piqué? We did not murmur at paying three shillings each,
my father, my mother and myself, in order to see *La Tour
de Nesle*, but the new tariff outraged our thrifty villagers,
and the troupe departed next day to pitch its tents at X.,
an aristocratic and coquettish little neighbouring town,
nestling at the foot of its castle, in obeisance before its
titled owners. *La Tour de Nesle* played to a full house, and
the Lady of the Manor bestowed public congratulations,
after the performance, upon Monsieur Marcel d'Avricourt, the lead, a tall, agreeable young man who fenced
like an angel and veiled his melting gazelle eyes under
thick lashes. The hall was packed to suffocation the
next night, when they gave *Denise*. On the following day,
a Sunday, Monsieur d'Avricourt, in a morning coat at the
eleven o'clock Mass, offered holy water to two blushing
young girls, and withdrew without so much as a glance
at their emotion—a discretion which all X. was still
extolling a few hours later, at the matinée of *Hernani*,
when people had to be turned away.

The wife of the young solicitor at X. was by no means
shy. She affected the youthful and impulsive whims of a
woman who copied the clothes of "The Ladies" of the
Manor, sang songs to her own accompaniment and wore
her hair in a bang. Early next morning she set out to
order a *vol-au-vent* at the Hôtel de la Poste, where Monsieur d'Avricourt was lodging, and to collect gossip from
the manageress.

"For eight people, then, madame? At seven o'clock on
Saturday without fail! I'll write down the order as soon
as I've poured out Monsieur d'Avricourt's hot milk. Yes,
madame, he's staying here. Indeed, madame, no one
would take him for an actor! A voice like a young

lady's. And as soon as he's taken his walk after luncheon, back he comes to his own room and his needlework."

"His needlework?"

"His embroidery, madame, he embroiders like an angel! He's doing a piano cover in satin-stitch that's fit for an exhibition! My daughter has copied the design."

The solicitor's wife lost no time. That very day, she spied Monsieur d'Avricourt meditating in the lime avenue, accosted him and enquired after a certain piano cover of which the design and execution were said to be . . . Monsieur d'Avricourt blushed, veiled his gazelle eyes with a slender hand, gave two or three odd little cries and shyly uttered a few words.

"Trifles! Mere trifles that are all the rage in Paris."

A gracefully affected gesture, as though flicking away a fly, finished the sentence, and the solicitor's wife responded by an invitation to tea.

"Just a little friendly tea-party to which we can all bring our needlework. . . ."

During the week *Le Gendre de Monsieur Poirier* was lauded to the skies, together with *Hernani*, *Le Bossu* and *Les Deux Timides*, by a public whose enthusiasm knew no bounds. The lady in the box office, the chemist's and the tax-collector's wives were deeply impressed by the tints of Monsieur d'Avricourt's ties, by his manner of walking, of bowing, of punctuating his crystalline laughter with little treble cries, of resting his hand on his hip as though on a sword-hilt—and most deeply of all, by his embroidery. The top-booted manager of the troupe basked in prosperity, despatching money orders to the *Crédit Lyonnais* and spending his afternoons at the *Café de la Perle*, together with the noble father, the large-nosed comic and the rather snub-nosed leading lady.

It was at this moment that the Lord of the Manor, who

had been away from home for a fortnight, returned from
Paris to seek advice from the solicitor at X. He found the
solicitor's wife dispensing tea. Beside her sat his senior
clerk, an ambitious bony giant, counting his stitches on
the tightly-stretched material of a tambour frame. The
chemist's son, a ruddy-faced little rip, was embroidering
a monogram on a tea-cloth, while Glaume, a portly and
eligible widower, was filling in the design on a slipper
with alternate squares of magenta and old gold wool.
Even trembling old Monsieur Demange was trying his
hand on a piece of coarse canvas. Standing before them,
Monsieur d'Avricourt was reciting verses; an incense of
sighs rose from the circle of idle women upon whom his
Oriental eyes disdained to rest.

I never knew exactly with what abrupt words, or
possibly by what even more crushing silence, the Lord of
the Manor withered "the rage of Paris" and brushed
the scales from the eyes of those good folk who
sat staring at him, needle in hand. But I have often heard
tell that early next morning the troupe struck camp, and
that at the Hôtel de la Poste there remained no trace
of Lagardère, Hernani or of Monsieur Poirier's im-
pertinent son-in-law—nothing save a skein of coloured
silk and a forgotten thimble.

THE LITTLE BOUILLOUX GIRL

THE little Bouilloux girl was so lovely that even we children noticed it. It is unusual for small girls to recognise beauty in one of themselves and pay homage to it. But there could be no disputing such undeniable loveliness as hers. Whenever my mother met the little Bouilloux girl in the street, she would stop her and bend over her as she was wont to bend over her yellow tea-rose, her red flowering cactus or her Azure Blue butterfly trustfully asleep on the scaly bark of the pine tree. She would stroke her curly hair, golden as a half-ripe chestnut, and her delicately tinted cheeks, and watch the incredible lashes flutter over her great dark eyes. She would observe the glimmer of the perfect teeth in her peerless mouth, and when, at last, she let the child go on her way, she would look after her, murmuring, "It's prodigious!"

Several years passed, bringing yet further graces to the little Bouilloux girl. There were certain occasions recorded by our admiration: a prize-giving at which, shyly murmuring an unintelligible recitation, she glowed through her tears like a peach under a summer shower. The little Bouilloux girl's first communion caused a scandal: the same evening, after vespers, she was seen drinking a half pint at the *Café du Commerce*, with her father, the sawyer, and that night she danced, already feminine and flirtatious, a little unsteady in her white slippers, at the public ball.

With an arrogance to which she had accustomed us, she informed us later, at school, that she was to be apprenticed.

"Oh! Who to?"

"To Madame Adolphe."

"Oh! And are you to get wages at once?"

"No. I'm only thirteen, I shall start earning next year."

She left us without emotion, and coldly we let her go. Already her beauty isolated her and she had no friends at school, where she learned very little. Her Sundays and her Thursdays brought no intimacy with us; they were spent with a family that was considered "unsuitable", with girl cousins of eighteen well known for their brazen behaviour, and with brothers, cartwright apprentices, who sported ties at fourteen and smoked when they escorted their sister to the Parisian shooting-gallery at the fair or to the cheerful bar that the widow Pimolle had made so popular.

The very next morning on my way to school I met the little Bouilloux girl setting out for the dressmaker's workrooms, and I remained motionless, thunderstruck with jealous admiration, at the corner of the Rue des Sœurs, watching Nana Bouilloux's retreating form. She had exchanged her black pinafore and short childish frock for a long skirt and a pleated blouse of pink sateen. She wore a black alpaca apron and her exuberant locks, disciplined and twisted into a "figure of eight", lay close as a helmet about the charming new shape of a round imperious head that retained nothing childish except its freshness and the not yet calculated impudence of a little village adventuress.

That morning the upper forms hummed like a hive.

"I've seen Nana Bouilloux! In a long dress, my dear, would you believe it? And her hair in a chignon! She had a pair of scissors hanging from her belt too!"

At noon I flew home to announce breathlessly:

"Mother! I met Nana Bouilloux in the street! She was passing our door. And she had on a long dress! Mother, just imagine, a long dress! And her hair in a chignon! And she had high heels and a pair of..."

"Eat, Minet-Chéri, eat, your cutlet will be cold."

"And an apron, mother, such a lovely alpaca apron that looked like silk! Couldn't I possibly..."

"No, Minet-Chéri you certainly couldn't."

"But if Nana Bouilloux can..."

"Yes, Nana Bouilloux, at thirteen, can, in fact she should, wear a chignon, a short apron and a long skirt— it's the uniform of all little Bouilloux girls throughout the world, at thirteen—more's the pity."

"But..."

"Yes, I know you would like to wear the complete uniform of a little Bouilloux girl. It includes all that you've seen, and a bit more besides: a letter safely hidden in the apron pocket, an admirer who smells of wine and of cheap cigars; two admirers, three admirers and a little later on plenty of tears... and a sickly child hidden away, a child that has lain for months crushed by constricting stays. There it is, Minet-Chéri, the entire uniform of the little Bouilloux girls. Do you still want it?"

"Of course not, mother. I only wanted to see if a chignon..."

But my mother shook her head, mocking but serious.

"No, no! You can't have the chignon without the apron, the apron without the letter, the letter without the high-heeled slippers, or the slippers without... all the rest of it! It's just a matter of choice!"

My envy was soon exhausted. The resplendent little Bouilloux girl became no more than a daily passer-by whom I scarcely noticed. Bareheaded in winter and summer, her gaily coloured blouses varied from week to week, and in very cold weather she swathed her elegant shoulders in a useless little scarf. Erect, radiant as a thorny rose, her eyelashes sweeping her cheeks or half revealing her dark and dewy eyes, she grew daily more worthy of queening it over crowds, of being gazed at, adorned and bedecked with jewels. The severely smoothed crinkliness of her chestnut hair could still be discerned in little waves that caught the light in the golden mist at the nape of her neck and round her ears. She always looked vaguely offended with her small, velvety nostrils reminding one of a doe.

She was fifteen or sixteen now—and so was I. Except that she laughed too freely on Sundays, in order to show her white teeth, as she hung on the arms of her brothers or her girl cousins, Nana Bouilloux was behaving fairly well.

"For a little Bouilloux girl, very well indeed!" was the public verdict.

She was seventeen, then eighteen; her complexion was like a peach on a south wall, no eyes could meet the challenge of hers and she had the bearing of a goddess. She began to take the floor at fêtes and fairs, to dance with abandon, to stay out very late at night, wandering in the lanes with a man's arm round her waist. Always unkind, but full of laughter, provoking boldness in those who would have been content merely to love her.

Then came a St. John's Eve when she appeared on the dance floor that was laid down on the *Place du Grand-Jeu* under the melancholy light of malodorous oil lamps. Hob-nailed boots kicked up the dust between the planks of the "floor". All the young men, as was customary, kept their hats on while dancing. Blonde girls became claret-coloured in their tight bodices, while the dark ones, sunburned from their work in the fields, looked black. But there, among a band of haughty workgirls, Nana Bouilloux, in a summer dress sprigged with little flowers, was drinking lemonade laced with red wine when the Parisians arrived on the scene.

They were two Parisians such as one sees in the country in summer, friends of a neighbouring landowner, and supremely bored; Parisians in tussore and white serge, come for a moment to mock at a village mid-summer fête. They stopped laughing when they saw Nana Bouilloux and sat down near the bar in order to see her better. In low voices they exchanged comments which she pretended not to hear, since her pride as a beautiful creature would not let her turn her eyes in their direction and giggle like her companions. She heard the words: "A swan among geese! A Greuze! A crime to let such a wonder bury herself here...." When the young man in the white suit asked the little Bouilloux girl for a waltz she got up without surprise and danced with him gravely, in silence. From time to time her eyelashes, more beautiful than a glance, brushed against her partner's fair moustache.

After the waltz the two Parisians went away, and Nana Bouilloux sat down by the bar, fanning herself. There she was soon approached by young Leriche, by Houette, even by Honce the chemist, and even by Possy the cabinet-maker, who was ageing, but none the less a good dancer. To all of them she replied, "Thank you, but I'm tired," and she left the ball at half-past ten o'clock.

And after that, nothing more ever happened to the little Bouilloux girl. The Parisians did not return, neither they, nor others like them. Houette, Honce, young Leriche, the commercial travellers with their gold watch-chains, soldiers on leave and sheriff's clerks vainly climbed our steep street at the hours when the beautifully coiffed sempstress, on her way down it, passed them by stiffly with a distant nod. They looked out for her at dances, where she sat drinking lemonade with an air of distinction and answered their importunities with "Thank you very much, but I'm not dancing, I'm tired." Taking offence, they soon began to snigger: "Tired! Her kind of tiredness lasts for thirty-six weeks!" and they kept a sharp watch on her figure. But nothing happened to the little Bouilloux girl, neither that nor anything else. She was simply waiting, possessed by an arrogant faith, conscious of the debt owed by the hazard that had armed her too well. She was awaiting... not the return of the Parisian in white serge, but a stranger, a ravisher. Her proud anticipation kept her silent and pure; with a little smile of surprise, she rejected Honce, who would have raised her to the rank of chemist's lawful wife, and she would have nothing to say to the sheriff's chief clerk. With never another lapse, taking back, once and for all, the smiles, the glances, the glowing bloom of her cheeks, the red young lips, the shadowy blue cleft of her breasts which she had so prodigally lavished on mere rustics, she awaited her kingdom and the prince without a name.

Years later, when I passed through my native village, I could not find the shade of her who had so lovingly refused me what she called "The uniform of little Bouilloux girls". But as the car bore me slowly, though not slowly enough—never slowly enough—up a street where I have now no reason to stop, a woman drew back to avoid the wheel. A slender woman, her hair well dressed in a bygone fashion, dressmaker's scissors hanging from a steel "châtelaine" on her black apron. Large, vindictive eyes, a tight mouth sealed by long silence, the sallow cheeks and temples of those who work by lamplight; a woman of forty-five or . . . Not at all; a woman of thirty-eight, a woman of my own age, of exactly my age, there was no room for doubt. As soon as the car allowed her room to pass, "the little Bouilloux girl" went on her way down the street, erect and indifferent, after one anxious, bitter glance had told her that the car did not contain the long-awaited ravisher.

TOUTOUQUE

B ROAD and squat as a four months' pigling, smooth-coated and yellow with a black mask, she looked more like a diminutive mastiff than a bulldog. Vandals had trimmed her shell-like ears into points and had cut her tail close to her behind. But no dog or woman in the world ever received, as her share of beauty, eyes that could be compared to those of Toutouque. When my elder brother, then a volunteer in the neighbouring county town, rescued her, by bringing her home. to us, from an idiotic order condemning to death all the barrack dogs, she bestowed upon us one glance of those eyes the colour of old Madeira, a glance hardly at all anxious, but full of perception and shining with a moisture like that of human tears. We were all conquered on the spot and Toutouque was allotted her ample place before the wood fire. Everyone—and especially I who was then a little girl—felt the charm of her nanny-like amiability, and her equable temper. She barked very seldom, a muffled and throaty bark, but she talked a great deal in other ways, expressing her opinion with a flashing smile of black lips and white teeth, slyly lowering her dusky lids over her mulatto woman's eyes. She learned our names, a hundred new words and the names of all the she-cats, as quickly as an intelligent child. She took us all to her heart, followed my mother to the butcher's, and accompanied me daily a part of the way to school. But she belonged only to my elder brother who had saved her from the bullet or the rope. She loved him with an intensity of love that made her self-conscious in his presence. For his sake she became foolish, bowing her head and positively asking for the torments that she waited for as rewards. She would lie on her back, exposing her belly studded with purplish teats upon which my brother would strum, pinching each in turn, the tune of Boccherini's *Minuet*. The rite demanded that at each pinch Toutouque— who never failed to respond—should utter a little yelp, at which my brother would exclaim severely: "Toutouque, you're singing out of tune! Begin again!" There was no cruelty involved, the merest touch drew from the ticklish Toutouque a series of varied and musical cries. The game ended, she would remain supine, asking for more!

My brother warmly reciprocated her devotion, and composed for her benefit those songs which burst from us in moments of unchecked childishness, queer jingles born of rhythm and repetitions of words blossoming in the innocent vacancies of the mind. One refrain lauded Toutouque for being

"Oh, yellow, yellow, yellow.
Inordinately yellow,
Oh, uttermost extremity of yellow. . . ."

Another song celebrated her massive build and named her three times over, "endearing cylinder", to the lively cadence of a military march. Then Toutouque would roar with laughter; in other words, she would bare every tooth in her nubbly jaw, lay back what remained of her clipped ears, and in default of a tail to wag would wag her weighty posterior. Whether asleep in the garden or gravely occupied in the kitchen, the Song of the Cylinder, chanted by my brother, would bring Toutouque straight to his feet, captivated by the familiar strains.

One day when Toutouque lay roasting herself, after dinner, upon the burning marble of the hearth, my brother, seated at the piano, incorporated the Song of the Cylinder, without words, in the overture he was reading at sight. The opening bars hovered over the animal's slumber like importunate flies. Her coat, smooth as that of a Jersey cow's, twitched here and there, and her ears . . . An energetic repetition—piano solo—half opened the eyes, full of human confusion, of the musical Toutouque, who rose to her feet and asked me clearly: "Haven't I heard that tune somewhere?" Then she turned to her ingenious tormentor who was persistently hammering out the favourite air, accepted from his hands this new magic, and went and sat close to' the piano in order to listen better, with the knowing yet mystified expression of a child trying to follow a conversation between grown up people.

Her gentleness was a rebuke to all teasing. She was given new-born kittens to lick and the puppies of stranger bitches. She kissed the hands of toddling infants and allowed young chickens to peck her. I was inclined to despise her for her over-fed convivial meekness until the day came when Toutouque, in due season, lost her heart to a gundog, a setter belonging to the local restaurant keeper. He was a big setter, endowed as are all setters with a "Second Empire" charm; a red-blond, long-haired and with luminous eyes, he lacked character but not distinction. His mate resembled him as a sister, but was nervous and subject to vapours. She uttered shrieks if a door was banged and wailed at the sound of the Angelus. For purely euphonic reasons their master had named them Black and Bianca.

This brief idyll brought me to a fuller knowledge of our Toutouque. Walking with her past the café, I saw the red-haired Bianca lying upon its threshold, her paws crossed, her uncurled ringlets curtaining her cheeks.

The two bitches exchanged a single glance, and Bianca fled behind the bar shrieking the shriek of the crushed paw. Toutouque had not stirred from my side, and her tipsy sentimental eye enquired with astonishment: "What can be the matter with her?"

"Let her alone," I replied. "You know she's half-crazy."

None of the household troubled about Toutouque's private affairs. She was free to come and go, to push the swing door with her nose, to pass the time of day with the butcher or to join my father at his game of écarté; no one feared that Toutouque would stray or that she would get into mischief. So when the restaurant keeper came to inform us, accusing Toutouque, that his bitch Bianca had received a torn ear, we all burst into derisive laughter, pointing to Toutouque, sprawling blissfully, and being clawed by an imperious kitten.

Next morning I had established myself, like a stylite, on the top of one of the pillars connected by the garden railings, and was preaching to an invisible multitude, when I heard approaching a babel of canine howls, dominated by the shrill and desperate voice of Bianca. Then she appeared, dishevelled and haggard, passed the corner of the Rue de la Roche and fled down the Rue des Vignes. At her heels there rolled, with incredible speed, a kind of bristling yellow monster, its legs alternately tucked under its belly and splayed out on all sides, like those of a frog, by the headlong fury of its advance—a yellow creature with a black mask garnished with teeth, bulging eyes and a purple tongue flecked with foam. It flashed past like a whirlwind and was gone, and while I hastened to descend from my column, I heard from afar the clash, the stormy snarling of a very brief encounter and once again the voice of the red bitch, sorely wounded.

I ran across the garden, reached the street door and stood still in amazement; Toutouque, the monster I had glimpsed, yellow and murderous, Toutouque was there, lying at my feet on the steps.

"Toutouque!"

She attempted her kind, fostering smile, but she was gasping and the whites of her eyes, streaked with blood-shot lines, looked as if they were bleeding.

"Toutouque! Is it possible?"

She got up, squirmed heavily and tried to change the subject, but the black lips, the tongue that sought to lick my fingers, still had on them red-gold hairs torn from Bianca.

"Oh! Toutouque! Toutouque!"

I could find no other words in which to express my dismay, my alarm and my astonishment at seeing an evil power, whose very name was unknown to my ten years, so transform the gentlest of creatures into a savage brute.

THE SPAHI'S CLOAK

THE Spahi's cloak, the black burnous embroidered with gold, the *chéchia*, the "set" composed of three oval miniatures—a locket and two earrings—surrounded by a wreath of tiny precious stones, the piece of genuine *peau d'Espagne* indelibly perfumed—all these were treasures that in the past were to me, as they were to my mother, objects of reverence.

"These are not playthings," she would say gravely, and with such an air that I would be tempted to think them toys indeed, but toys for grown up people.

She would sometimes amuse herself by draping me in the thin black burnous, with its stripes of gold thread, and putting on my head the tasselled hood; at such times she would pat herself on the back for having given me birth.

"You shall have it as an evening cloak when you're married," she would say. "Nothing is more becoming, and at any rate it isn't a garment that goes out of fashion. Your father brought it back from his African campaign, together with the Spahi's cloak."

The Spahi's cloak, red, and of fine cloth, slept folded in an old, worn sheet, and my mother had slipped among its folds a cigar cut into four pieces and a seasoned meerschaum pipe as precautions "against the moth".

Did the moth become immunised, or did the seasoning in the pipe, in time, lose its insecticidal virtue? During one of those household upheavals that are known as spring cleanings, and which, surging through cupboards, break the seals of linen, paper and string like a river breaking up its ice, my mother unfolded the Spahi's cloak, and uttered a great cry of distress:

"It's been eaten!"

The family gathered round, as though round the remains of a cannibal feast, and examined the cloak which let in daylight through a hundred little holes, as round as though the fine cloth had been riddled with small shot.

"Eaten!" repeated my mother. "And my red fox fur, beside it, quite untouched!"

"Eaten," agreed my father with composure. "Well, there it is, it's been eaten."

My mother drew herself up before him, like a thrifty fury.

"You seem ready enough to accept the fact."

"Why, yes," said my father. "I've already got over it."

"Well, of course, you men . . ."

"Yes, I know. But what did you mean to do with that cloak?"

She lost her assurance on the spot and displayed the perplexity of a cat that is offered milk in a narrow-necked bottle.

"Why . . . I was keeping it! It's been in the same sheet for fifteen years. Twice a year I unfolded it, shook it out and folded it up again. . . ."

"Well, you're quit of that task, anyway. You can give your attention to the green tartan plaid, since we all know that the family is allowed to use the red-and-white one, but that no one must presume to touch the green one with the blue and yellow squares."

"I always put the green one over the little one's legs when she's ill."

"That's not true."

"Not true? What do you mean?"

"It isn't true, because she's never ill."

Quickly a hand sheltered my head as though the tiles of the roof were about to fall on it.

"Don't change the subject. What am I to do with this moth-eaten cloak? Such a big cloak! Five yards at the very least!"

"Good Heavens, my darling, if you feel so badly about it, fold it up again, pin its little shroud round it and put it back in the cupboard—just as though it weren't moth-eaten at all!"

My mother's quick flush rose to the cheeks that were still so smooth.

"Oh! How can you suggest such a thing! It wouldn't be the same! I couldn't do it. It would almost seem like . . ."

"Then, my darling, give me the cloak. I've got an idea."

"What are you going to do with it?"

"Never mind. I tell you I've got an idea."

She gave him the cloak, her perfect trust visible in her grey eyes. Had he not successively assured her that he knew how to make chocolate caramels of a certain kind, that he could economise half the corks when bottling a cask of claret, and kill the mole-crickets that were making havoc among our lettuces? That the badly-corked wine was spoilt in six months, that the caramel-making should have resulted in burning a yard of the flooring, and the crystal-lisation in boiling sugar of an entire suit of clothes; that the lettuces, poisoned by a mysterious acid, should have predeceased the mole-crickets—none of this was evidence that my father had been mistaken.

She gave him the Spahi's cloak, which he threw over his shoulder and bore away to his lair, otherwise known as the library. I followed up the stairs the quick step of his one leg, that crow's hop that hoisted him from step to step. But once in the library, he sat down, ordered me tersely to put within his reach a foot-rule, gum, the big scissors, a pair of compasses and some pins, turned me out of the room and bolted the door.

"What is he doing? Go and have a look at what he's doing," urged my mother.

But we knew nothing until the evening, when at last a vigorous call from my father brought us upstairs.

"Well," enquired my mother as she entered, "have you succeeded?"

"Look!"

He held out his hand triumphantly, and there on its palm—pinked like the teeth of a wolf, foliated like puff pastry and no bigger than a rose—lay all that remained of the Spahi's cloak: an elegant pen-wiper.

THE FRIEND

ON the day that the Opéra Comique was burnt down, my elder brother and another student, his best friend, had tried to get two seats. But other impecunious enthusiasts had exhausted the three franc seats and there was nothing left. The two disappointed students dined on the terrace of a small restaurant near by; an hour later, two hundred yards from where they were sitting, the Opéra Comique went up in flames. Before parting in haste, my brother to reassure my mother by telegram and the other to rejoin his family in Paris, the two friends clasped hands and looked each other in the eyes with the embarrassment and awkwardness under which very young men disguise their purest emotions. Neither of them spoke of providential good luck or of the mysterious protection that had hovered over their two heads. But that year, when the long vacation arrived, for the first time Maurice—we will suppose that his name was Maurice—accompanied my brother and came to spend two months under our roof. I was then a tallish little girl, about thirteen years old.

And that was how I first met Maurice, for whom I nourished a blind admiration on the strength of the affection my brother bore him. During the past two years I had already learnt that Maurice was studying law— which meant to me much the same as if they had told me that he was learning to sit up and beg—, that he shared my brother's passion for music, that he resembled in appearance the baritone, Taskin, with a moustache and a very small pointed beard, and that his wealthy parents were wholesale dealers in chemical products with an income of not less than fifty thousand francs a year—I am speaking, of course, of a long past epoch.

He arrived, and my mother lost no time in exclaiming that he was a hundred thousand times better looking than his photographs and even that he outdid all that my brother had boasted of him over the past two years: he was polished in manner with melting eyes, beautiful hands, a moustache tinged with auburn, and the beguiling ways of a son who has seldom left his mother. For my part I said nothing, for the simple reason that I whole-heartedly shared my mother's enthusiasm.

He arrived in a blue suit and a panama with a striped band, bringing me sweets, garnet, old-gold, and peacock-green monkeys made of silk chenille—the mascots of the moment, that a tiresome craze stuck on to everything—and a little turquoise-blue plush purse. But what cared I for presents in comparison with the treasures that I pilfered? I pinched from him and my brother everything upon which I could lay my sentimental little magpie claws: improper illustrated papers, Turkish cigarettes, cough lozenges, a pencil whose end bore the marks of teeth, and best of all, empty matchboxes, of a kind new at that time, decorated with the photographs of actresses whose names I was quick to memorise and to repeat without a blunder: Théo, Sybil Sanderson, Van Zandt. They belonged to an unknown, enviable race, invariably dowered by nature with huge eyes, very black lashes, hair curled in a fringe on the forehead, one bare shoulder and the other veiled by a wisp of tulle. Hearing them casually mentioned by Maurice, I collected them all in a harem under his indolent dominion, and at night, when I was going to bed, I practised the effect of one of mother's veils draped over my shoulder. For a full week I was cantankerous, jealous, pale and full of blushes— in other words, I was in love.

And then, since I was, after all is said and done, a very sensible little girl, the period of exaltation faded and I entered into full enjoyment of Maurice's friendship and good humour, and the free-and-easy conversation of the two friends. A more intelligent desire to please took control of my actions, and I became, with every appearance of simplicity, exactly what I needed to be in order to attract: a tall child with long plaits and a slim waist in a ribbon-belt, looking out like a watchful cat from the semi-eclipse of my big straw hat. I was seen again in the kitchen kneading dough for the cakes, or in the garden with my foot on a spade, and when the two friends went for country rambles, arm in arm, I hovered round them, like a loyal and graceful guardian angel. What lovely hot summer holidays those were, so full of emotion and so pure!

It was while listening to the conversation of the two young men that I learned of Maurice's impending, though still fairly distant, marriage. One day when we were alone in the garden I plucked up enough courage to ask him to show me a photograph of his future bride. He produced one of a pretty, smiling young girl, with an elaborate coiffure and a mass of lace frills swirling round her.

"Oh!" I exclaimed clumsily, "What a lovely dress!"

He laughed so spontaneously that I did not apologise.

"And what are you going to do when you're married?"

He stopped laughing and looked at me.

"How do you mean, what am I going to do? I shall soon be a barrister, you know!"

"Yes, I do know. But what will she do, your wife, while you're being a barrister?"

"How funny you are! Why, she'll be my wife!"

"You mean, she'll wear other frocks with lots of little frills?"

"She'll look after our house and receive our friends. Are you laughing at me? You know very well how one lives when one is married."

"No, not very well. But I do know how we've lived during the past six weeks."

"Who d'you mean by 'we'?"

"You, my brother and I. Do you like it here? Have you been happy? Are you fond of us?"

He raised his dark eyes to the slate roof with its patches of yellow lichen, and the wistaria in its second blooming; then he gazed at me a moment and murmured half to himself:

"Yes, of course."

"And later, when you're married, I don't suppose you'll be able to come back here for the holidays? You won't ever again be able to go for long rambles with my brother, holding my two plaits as if they were reins?"

I was trembling all over but I did not take my eyes from his face. His expression changed. He looked all round him, and then appeared to take stock, from head to foot, of the child who leaned against a tree looking up at him as she spoke, because she was still not tall enough. I remember his smiling slightly, as though it cost him an effort, and then he shrugged his shoulders and said rather foolishly:

"Why, no, I suppose not. That goes without saying. . . ."

He turned towards the house and left me without another word, and for the first time in my life there mingled, with the big childish sorrow I felt at losing Maurice, the faintly melancholy savour of a triumph that was more mature.

I HAVE forgotten his name. Why does his sad face sometimes emerge in the dreams that take me back at night to the time and place that knew my childhood? Can it be that his sad face wanders among the friendless dead, just as he wandered friendless among the living?

His name was something like Goussard, Voussard, or perhaps Gaumeau. He obtained the position of forwarding clerk with Maître Defert, the notary, and there he remained for years and years. But my village, which had not seen the birth of Voussard—or Gaumeau—, refused to adopt him. Even in extreme old age Voussard failed to graduate as a native. Tall, grey, thin and desiccated, he never sought to make friends, and even Rouillard, the violinist who kept the café and whose heart was softened by years of playing at the head of rustic wedding processions, never unbent towards him.

Voussard "fed" at Patasson's. "Feeding" at any particular place, in our village parlance, meant that one slept there also. Sixty francs a month inclusive: Voussard was in no danger of losing his figure, which remained lean, clad in a shiny jacket and a yellow waistcoat darned with coarse black thread. Yes, darned with coarse thread, just above the watch pocket, I can see it now. If I were a painter, I could paint a portrait of Voussard, twenty-five years after his disappearance, that would be inconceivably like him. Why? I have no idea. That waistcoat with its black-thread darns, that white paper that collar and that tie, a rag with a Paisley pattern. And above them that face, grey in the mornings like a dirty windowpane, because

Voussard left without breakfast, and blotched with a faint
redness after the midday meal. A long face, beardless but
always ill-shaven. A wide mouth, tight-lipped, ugly. A
long, greedy nose, with more flesh to it than the whole
face, and eyes . . . I only once saw his eyes, for they
generally sought the ground, besides being shadowed by a
black straw boater, too small for Voussard's head, which
he wore tilted forward on his forehead like the hats worn
by women during the Second Empire, at the period of the
"chignon Benoiton".

During the after-lunch hour of cognac and cigarettes,
Voussard, who did without both coffee and tobacco,
took the air a few paces from his office, on one of the two
stone benches that must still be standing on either side
of Madame Lachassagne's house. He would return there
towards four o'clock, when the rest of the village was
having its tea. The left-hand bench wore out the trouser
seats of Maître Defert's two clerks. In fine weather the
right-hand bench, at that hour, was jostled by a tight-
packed row of little girls already quite big, crowded
together and fidgeting like sparrows on the ledge of a
warm chimney: Odile, Yvonne, Marie, Colette. We were
thirteen or fourteen years old, the age of premature
putting up of hair, of leather belts tightened to the last
hole, of the painfully cramped shoe and the bang of hair
—"Well, that's that, can't be helped if mother doesn't
like it!"—cut at school during the sewing class, with the
aid of embroidery scissors. We were slender, sunburnt,
affected and ruthless, clumsy as boys, impudent, blushing
crimson at the mere sound of our own voices, ill-natured,
graceful, insufferable.

For some moments, sitting on the bench before school,
we posed for the benefit of anyone who might be walking
down from the heights of Bel-Air; but we never looked at

Voussard, hunched over his folded newspaper. Our
mothers were vaguely afraid of him:

"You haven't been sitting on that bench again, so near
that creature?"

"What creature, mother?"

"The man from Defert's. I don't like to think of it!"

"But why, mother?"

"I have my own reasons."

He inspired them with the horror that one has for a
satyr, or for a silent madman who may suddenly become
homicidal. But Voussard appeared unconscious of our
presence and we never even thought of him as alive.

In place of dessert he nibbled a sprig of lime, crossing
his skinny shanks with the ease of a frivolous skeleton,
and reading his paper in the shadow of his dusty black
straw hat. At half past twelve, little Ménétreau, formerly
the school errand-boy and recently promoted to be
office-boy in Defert's office, sat himself down beside
Voussard, and devoured his midday crust like a terrier
demolishing a slipper. From over Madame Lachassagne's
wall, flowers drifted down upon us all, wistaria and labur-
num, the scent of lime trees, the open blossom of a
clematis spinning slowly round, red berries of yew. . . .
Odile would affect a fit of the giggles to attract a passing
commercial traveller; Yvonne would be watching for the
new assistant master to appear at the window of upper-
form classroom, and I would be scheming to put my
piano out of tune in order that the tuner from the county
town, who wore gold pince-nez . . . Voussard would
read on like an automaton.

There came a day when little Ménétreau was the first
to arrive at the left-hand bench, to sit there munching the
remains of his bread and popping down cherries. Voussard
came late just as the school bell was ringing. He was

walking quickly and awkwardly, like somebody hurrying in the dark, and from his fingers dangled an open newspaper which brushed the street. He laid a hand on little Ménétreau's shoulder, bent down and announced in deep and hurried tones:

"Ybañez is dead. They've assassinated him."

Little Ménétreau opened a mouth full of chewed bread and stuttered: "No . . . not really?"

"Yes. The king's soldiers. Look."

Tragically he unfolded the newspaper and with trembling fingers thrust it under the office boy's nose.

"Ah, well!" sighed little Ménétreau. "I wonder what will happen now?"

"As if I could tell you!" Voussard's great arms were flung heavenwards and fell to his sides.

"This is Cardinal Richelieu's doing," he added with a bitter laugh.

Then he took off his hat, wiped his forehead and remained a moment motionless, sweeping the valley with those eyes we did not know, the yellow eyes of an island conqueror, the cruel, far-gazing eyes of a pirate on the look-out under his black flag, the despairing eyes of the faithful comrade of Ybañez, basely done to death by "the King's men".

MY MOTHER AND THE CURÉ

HERSELF an unbeliever, my mother allowed me to
attend catechism classes when I was eleven or
twelve years old. The only obstacles she put in my way
were her caustic comments, uttered with shattering
candour every time she came across a humble little
manual bound in blue boards. She would open the
catechism at random and lose her temper on the spot.

"Oh, how I dislike this system of cross-examination!
'What is God?' What is this? What is that? All these
question marks, this mania for interrogation and in-
quisition, I find that incredibly indiscreet! And then the
commandments, I ask you! Who in the world ever translated them into such gibberish? Oh dear, I don't like
seeing this book in a child's hands; it's full of such unsuitable and complicated things."

"Then take it away from your daughter," my father
would reply. "That's quite easy."

"Not as easy as you think. It isn't only a question of
the catechism! There's confession as well to be thought
of. And that really beats all! It makes me red with anger
even to speak of it. Look how red I am!"

"Then don't speak of it."

"Oh! You. . . . Your philosophy's so simple: 'If a
thing's tiresome, don't think about it and it ceases to
exist!' Isn't that it?"

"I couldn't put it better."

"It's all very well joking, that's no answer. I can't
reconcile myself to the questions they ask this child."

"! ! !"

"It's all very well to look so incredulous! It's perfectly

awful, this system of revealing, confessing, re-confessing and displaying every fault one commits! Better far hold one's tongue and punish oneself inwardly. That's what they ought to teach. Confession only accustoms a child to wordy effervescence, to an intimate soul-searching that soon has in it much more of complacent vanity than humility, I can assure you! I don't like it at all, and I'm going to step round this very minute to give the Curé a bit of my mind!"

She threw round her shoulders her best black, cashmere, jet-beaded pelisse, put on her little bonnet trimmed with bunches of purple lilac, and with her inimitable sprightly gait—toes turned out, heels barely touching the ground—step round she did, to ring the bell at Monsieur le Curé's door, a hundred yards away. I could hear, from our house, its sad crystalline tinkle, and I sat uncomfortably visualising a dramatic encounter, with threats and abuse, between my mother and the parish priest. My romantic child's heart thumped painfully at the bang of the closing front door. But my mother reappeared wreathed in smiles and my father, lowering *Le Temps* before his face, bushy as a forest landscape, enquired:

"Well?"

"Very well indeed!" was my mother's quick rejoinder. "I've got him!"

"The Curé?"

"No, of course not! The pelargonium cutting he was guarding so jealously; you know, the one that has two deep purple petals and three pink ones! Here he is. I'm going to pot him at once."

"But did you dress him down about the child?"

My mother, on the edge of the terrace, gaily turned towards us a charming, flushed face of innocent surprise:

"Certainly not! What an idea! You haven't an ounce

of tact! A man who's not only given me the pelargonium cutting, but has also promised me his Spanish honey-suckle—the one that has leaves variegated with white that we can smell from here when there's a westerly wind. . . ."

She was already out of sight, but her voice still reached us, a brisk, soprano voice full of inflexions that trembled at the slightest emotion and proclaimed, to all and sundry, news of delicate plants, of graftings, of rain and blossomings, like the voice of a hidden bird that foretells the weather.

On Sundays she seldom missed Mass. In winter she took her foot-warmer, in summer her parasol; in all seasons a large black prayer-book and her dog Domino, who by turns was a mongrel black-and-white fox-terrier-spitz and a yellow water-spaniel.

The aged Curé Millot, almost subjugated by my mother's voice, her imperious kindness and her scandalous sincerity, ventured none the less to suggest that Mass was not said for dogs.

She bristled like a belligerent hen.

"My dog! Turn my dog out of church! What are you afraid he may learn there?"

"It isn't a question of . . ."

"My dog who is a model of deportment! A dog that gets up and lies down in unison with your congregation!"

"All that is true enough, my dear lady, but you can't deny that last Sunday he growled during the Elevation!"

"But of course he growled during the Elevation! I should be very much surprised if he didn't growl during the Elevation! Haven't I trained him myself to be a watch-dog and to bark whenever he hears a bell!"

The great battle of the dog in church, punctuated by truces and acute crises, lasted a long time, but the final victory remained with my mother. At eleven o'clock, with her dog in attendance—a very well-behaved dog, it must be added—she would shut herself into the family pew, just underneath the pulpit, with that slightly forced and childish gravity which she was wont to assume as a Sunday garment. The holy water, the sign of the Cross—she forgot nothing, not even the appropriate genuflexions.

"And how can you tell, Monsieur le Curé, whether I'm praying or not? It's true I don't know the 'Pater Noster', but that doesn't take long to learn—or to forget either, for that matter. But during Mass, when you compel us to remain on our knees, I get a few quiet moments in which to think over my problems. It strikes me that the little one isn't looking very fit, and that I'll get up a bottle of Château-Larose to put some colour into her cheeks. That those unhappy Pluviers are going to bring yet another child into the world without swaddling clothes or nappies unless I take a hand. That to-morrow is washing day and that I must get up at four o'clock."

He would hold up a weather-beaten gardener's hand to stem the torrent. "That's all right, that's all right. It shall all be counted to you as prayer."

During Mass she would study a black leather volume, with a cross stamped on either side of its binding; she would become so absorbed in its contents that her piety appeared astonishing to those friends of my very dear infidel who did not know that the sacred binding concealed a pocket edition of the plays of Corneille.

But sermon time transformed my mother into a devil incarnate. Neither the mistakes in pronunciation, nor the slips of the tongue, nor the Christian simplicities of an old peasant, could make her relent. Nervous yawns escaped from her like spurts of flame; and she confided to me in undertones the details of a thousand ailments that suddenly assailed her:

"My stomach's fluttering. I know that means there's an attack of palpitations coming on. Don't I look very flushed? I'm afraid I'm going to faint. I shall have to forbid Monsieur Millot to preach for more than ten minutes."

She informed him of her latest ultimatum, and this time he sent her about her business. But on the following Sunday, during the sermon, once the ten minutes had elapsed, she contrived to cough, drop her book, and swing her watch ostentatiously at the end of its chain.

Monsieur le Curé tried to ignore her, but he lost both his head and the trend of his sermon. Stammering an unexpected and misplaced "Amen," he left the pulpit, blessing, with a bewildered gesture, his whole flock, not excepting that rebellious lamb who sat immediately below him, her laughing face alight with the insolence of a reprobate.

MY MOTHER AND MORALS

WHEN I was thirteen or fourteen years old I was not socially inclined. Whenever my elder half-brother, the medical student, came home for the holidays, he taught me his quiet, systematic unsociability, unremitting as the vigilance of wild beasts. A ring at the front door bell would project him with a silent leap into the garden, and in bad weather the rambling house offered many a refuge for the pleasures of solitude. By instinct or imitation, I knew how to get through the kitchen window, climb over the spiked railings into the Rue des Vignes, and melt into the shadow of the lofts so soon as a ring at the bell was followed by amiable female voices raised in the sing-song of our native province. And yet I enjoyed the visits of Madame Saint-Alban, a still-handsome woman crowned by naturally curly hair, which she wore in swathes that quickly became dishevelled. She resembled George Sand and all her movements bore the stamp of a certain gipsy majesty. Her warm tawny eyes reflected the sunshine and the green trees, and in my infancy I had been suckled at her abundant swarthy breast, on a day when my mother jestingly offered her white breast to a little Saint-Alban of my age.

To visit my mother, Madame Saint-Alban would leave her house at the corner of our street and her narrow garden where the clematis grew pale in the shadow of the thuyas. Or perhaps she would call on her way home from a ramble, laden with wild honeysuckle, purple heather, mint from the marshes and flowering bulrushes, velvety brown and rough to the touch as sea-urchins. Her oval brooch was used often enough to draw together a rent in her black taffeta gown, and her little finger was adorned by a red cornelian heart engraved with the words *"je brusle, je brusle"*, an antique ring picked up in the open fields.

I think I was chiefly attracted to Madame Saint-Alban by all those things in her that least resembled my mother, and I savoured with thoughtful sensuality their mingled perfumes. Madame Saint-Alban gave forth a heavy dark aroma, the incense of her frizzy hair and suntanned arms. My mother smelled of laundered cretonne, of irons heated on the poplar-wood fire, of lemon-verbena leaves which she rolled between her palms or thrust into her pocket. At nightfall I used to imagine that she smelled of newly-watered lettuces, for the refreshing scent of them would follow her footsteps to the rippling sound of the rain from the watering-can, in a glory of spray and tillable dust.

I also enjoyed listening to the village chronicle as recorded by Madame Saint-Alban. Her narratives hung upon each familiar name a kind of disastrous escutcheon, a weather forecast announcing to-morrow's adultery, next week's ruin, or an incurable disease. A generous fire would then light up her tawny eyes, an enthusiastic and impartial malignity exalt her, and I could scarcely refrain from crying aloud: "Encore! Encore!"

Sometimes in my presence she would lower her voice. All the richer for being but half understood, the mysterious scandal would be spread over several days, the flame skilfully fanned and then suddenly quenched. I particularly remember the "Bonnarjaud story".

Scions of a mythical or rustic nobility, Monsieur and Madame de Bonnarjaud struggled to make ends meet in a small castle whose surrounding demesne, after repeated sales, was reduced to a walled-in park. No money and three marriageable daughters. "The de Bonnarjaud young ladies" came to Mass in revealing frocks. Would anyone ever marry "the de Bonnarjaud young ladies"?

"Sido! Guess what's happened!" cried Madame Saint-Alban one morning. "The second Bonnarjaud girl is getting married!"

She had come from visiting the farms scattered around the little castle, and she arrived bearing her usual spoils of gossip, her sheaves of green oats, poppies and corn-flowers, and early foxgloves from the stony combes. A transparent jade-green spinner-caterpillar hung from its silken thread beneath Madame Saint-Alban's ear, and the poplars had bestowed a beard of silver pollen on her sunburnt chin that was moist with perspiration.

"Sit down, Adrienne, and you shall have a glass of my red-currant syrup. As you see, I'm busy tying up my nasturtiums. The second Bonnarjaud girl? The one with rather a weak leg? I can't help suspecting some kind of wire-pulling in all that! But the life of those three girls is sad and empty enough to wring one's heart. Boredom is so intensely depraving! What principles could be proof against boredom?"

"Oh, you! If you begin spouting morality, God only knows where we shall end! Moreover, there is no question here of any ridiculous alliance. She's marrying . . . I'll give you a hundred guesses! Gaillard du Gougier!"

Quite unimpressed, my mother pursed her lips.

"Gaillard du Gougier! Really! A fine match, I must say!"

"The best-looking young man in the neighbourhood! All the eligible girls are crazy about him."

"Why say 'about him'? You need only say, 'All the eligible girls are crazy!' However. . . . When is it to be?"

"Ah! That's just it!"

"I somehow fancied there'd be a hitch somewhere. . . ."

"The Bonnarjauds are waiting for the death of an old aunt whose entire fortune goes to the three girls. If she dies, of course they'll look higher than du Gougier! And that's how things stand at present."

A week later we learned that the Gougiers and the Bonnarjauds were giving each other the cold shoulder. A month passed, and, the great-aunt having departed this life, the Baron de Bonnarjaud kicked du Gougier out of the house "like a lackey". Finally, at the end of summer, Madame Saint-Alban, looking like a bohemian Pomona trailing wreaths of ruddy vines and masses of meadow saffron, arrived in a high state of excitement and poured into my mother's ear a few words that I was unable to catch.

"No?" exclaimed my mother. Then she reddened with indignation.

"What are they going to do?" she enquired after a moment's silence.

Madame Saint-Alban shrugged her handsome shoulders draped with viburnum.

"What are they going to do? Why, marry them off in two seconds, of course! What else could the worthy Bonnarjauds do? From what I hear, they're three months late already! It seems that Gaillard du Gougier used to meet the girl at night, quite close to the house, in the little pavilion that . . ."

"And Madame de Bonnarjaud intends to give him her daughter?"

Madame Saint-Alban laughed like a Bacchante.

"Oh, come now! And thankful enough, I imagine! What would you do in her shoes?"

My mother's grey eyes sought me and dwelt upon me severely.

"What would I do? I should say to my daughter: 'Carry your burden, my child, not far from me, but far from that man, and never see him again! Or if by any chance the evil desire still has you in its grip, seek him at night, in the pavilion. Hide your shameful enjoyment. But never allow that man to pass our threshold in daylight, a man who was capable of taking you in the dark, under the windows of your sleeping parents. To sin and scourge oneself, to sin and then drive forth the unworthy one, is not irreparable shame. Your ruin begins from the moment when you consent to become the wife of a knave; your fault lies in hoping that the man who has stolen you away from your own hearth has a hearth of his own to offer you'."

LAUGHTER

SHE was easily moved to laughter, a youthful, rather shrill laughter that brought tears to her eyes, and which she would afterwards deplore as inconsistent with the dignity of a mother burdened with the care of four children and financial worries. She would master her paroxysms of mirth, scolding herself severely, "Come, now, come! . . ." and then fall to laughing again till her pince-nez trembled on her nose.

We would jealously compete in our efforts to evoke her laughter, especially as we grew old enough to observe in her face, as the years succeeded each other, the ever-increasing shadow of anxiety for the morrow, a kind of distress which sobered her whenever she thought of the fate of her penniless children, of her precarious health, of old age that was slowing the steps—a single leg and two crutches—of her beloved companion. When she was silent, my mother resembled all mothers who are scared at the thought of poverty and death. But speech brought back to her features an invincible youthfulness. Though she might grow thin with sorrow, she never spoke sadly. She would escape, as it were in one bound, from a painful reverie, and pointing her knitting needle at her husband would exclaim:

"What? Just you try to die first, and you'll see!"

"I shall do my best, dear heart," he would answer.

She would glare at him as savagely as if he had carelessly trodden on a pelargonium cutting or broken the little gold-enamelled Chinese teapot.

"Isn't that just like you! You've got all the selfishness

of the Funels and the Colettes combined! Oh, why did
I ever marry you?"

"Because, my beloved, I threatened to blow out your
brains if you didn't."

"True enough. Even in those days, you see, you
thought only of yourself! And now here you are talking
of nothing less than of dying before me. All I say is,
only let me see you try!"

He did try, and succeeded at the first attempt. He died
in his seventy-fourth year, holding the hands of his
beloved, and fixing on her weeping eyes a gaze that
gradually lost its colour, turned milky blue and faded like
a sky veiled in mist. He was given the handsomest of
village funerals, a coffin of yellow wood covered only by
an old tunic riddled with wounds—the tunic he had worn
as a captain in the 1st Zouaves—and my mother accompanied him steadily to the grave's edge, very small and
resolute beneath her widow's veil, and murmuring under
her breath words of love that only he must hear.

We brought her back to the house, and there she
promptly lost her temper with her new mourning, the
cumbersome crape that caught on the keys of doors and
presses, the cashmere dress that stifled her. She sat resting
in the drawing-room, near the big green chair in which
my father would never sit again and which the dog had
already joyfully invaded. She was dry-eyed, flushed and
feverish and kept on repeating:

"Oh, how hot it is! Heavens! The heat of this black
stuff! Don't you think I might change now, into my blue
sateen?"

"Well . . ."

"Why not? Because of my mourning? But I simply
loathe black! For one thing, it's melancholy. Why
should I present a sad and unpleasant sight to everyone I

meet? What connection is there between this cashmere and crape and my feelings? Don't let me ever see you in mourning for me! You know well enough that I only like you to wear pink, and some shades of blue."

She got up hastily, took several steps towards an empty room and stopped abruptly:

"Ah! . . . Of course. . . ."

She came back and sat down again, admitting with a simple and humble gesture that she had, for the first time that day, forgotten that *he* was dead.

"Shall I get you something to drink, mother? Wouldn't you like to go to bed?"

"Of course not. Why should I? I'm not ill!"

She sat there and began to learn patience, staring at the floor, where a dusty track from the door of the sitting-room to the door of the empty bedroom had been marked by rough, heavy shoes.

A kitten came in, circumspect and trustful, a common and irresistible little kitten four or five months old. He was acting a dignified part for his own edification, pacing grandly, his tail erect as a candle, in imitation of lordly males. But a sudden and unexpected somersault landed him head over heels at our feet, where he took fright at his own temerity, rolled himself into a ball, stood up on his hind legs, danced sideways, arched his back, and then spun round like a top.

"Look at him, oh, do look at him, Minet-Chéri! Goodness! Isn't he funny!"

And she laughed, sitting there in her mourning, laughed her shrill, young girl's laugh, clapping her hands with delight at the kitten. Then, of a sudden, searing memory stemmed that brilliant cascade and dried the tears of laughter in my mother's eyes. Yet she offered no excuse for having laughed, either on that day, or on the days that followed; for though she had lost the man she passionately loved, in her kindness for us she remained among us just as she always had been, accepting her sorrow as she would have accepted the advent of a long and dreary season, but welcoming from every source the fleeting benediction of joy. So she lived on, swept by shadow and sunshine, bowed by bodily torments, resigned, unpredictable and generous, rich in children, flowers and animals like a fruitful domain.

MY MOTHER AND ILLNESS

"WHAT time is it? Eleven o'clock already! Didn't I say so? He'll be here in a minute. Give me the eau-de-Cologne and the rough towel. And give me the little bottle of violet scent too. Violet scent, did I call it! There isn't any real violet scent nowadays. They make it with orris-root. Or do they even use that? But you don't care about that, Minet-Chéri, you don't like violet essence. What's come over our daughters that they don't like violet essence any more?

"Time was when a really refined woman never used any scent but violet. That stuff you drench yourself with isn't respectable. You simply use it to put people off the scent. Yes, that's exactly it, to put them on the wrong scent! Your short hair, the blue you put on your eyelids, the eccentricities you indulge in on the stage—its all, just like your perfume, to put people on the wrong scent. Yes it is, it's so that they will think you an unusual person with no prejudices. . . . Poor Minet-Chéri! But you don't take me in. . . . Undo my two wretched little plaits. I did them up very tightly last night so that I would have a wave this morning. D'you know what I look like? An elderly indigent poet with no talent. It's mighty difficult to retain the characteristics of one's sex after a certain age. In my decline, two things distress me: that I can no longer wash my little blue saucepan for boiling milk myself, and the sight of my own hand on the sheet. You'll understand later that one keeps on forgetting old age up to the very brink of the grave.

"Even illness can't force one to remember it. Every hour I say to myself: 'I've a pain in my back. The nape of

my neck aches atrociously. I've no appetite. That digitalis
goes to my head and makes me feel sick! I'm going to
die, to-night, to-morrow, no matter when. . . .' But I'm
not always thinking of the ways in which age has altered
me, and it's when I look at my hand that I realise the
change. I'm astonished not to see under my eyes my little
hand as it was when I was twenty. . . . Hush! Be quiet a
moment and let me listen. I hear singing. . . . Ah! It's
old Madame Lœuvrier's funeral. A good job they're
burying her at last! No, no, I'm not a brute! I say 'a good
job' because she won't any longer be able to bother her
poor fool of a daughter, who is fifty-five and has never
dared to get married, for fear of her mother. Ah! Parents!
I do say it's a good job that there should be one old lady
the less on this earth.

"No, decidedly, I can't accustom myself to old age,
neither my own nor other people's. And, seeing I'm
seventy-one, I'd better give up trying as I shall never
succeed. Be a darling, Minet-Chéri, and push my bed
nearer the window so that I can see old Madame Lœuvrier go by. I adore watching funerals pass, one can always
learn something from them. What a crowd! That's
because of the fine weather. It's a good excuse for a
pleasant walk. If it had rained, she'd have had three cats
for an escort, and Monsieur Miroux wouldn't have risked
wetting that fine black-and-silver cope. And what heaps
of flowers! Oh, the vandals! They've simply massacred the
saffron rose-tree in the Lœuvrier's garden. Fancy killing
all those young flowers for the sake of an old woman.

"And look, look at that great idiot of a daughter; I was
sure of it, she's crying her heart out. Of course, that's only
common sense; she has lost her torturer, her tormentor,
the daily poison, the lack of which may well kill her.
After her come what I call the vultures. Oh, those faces!

There are days when I congratulate myself that I haven't got a cent to leave you. The very thought that I might be followed to my last home by a great red-headed lout like that nephew there; look at him—he'll spend his time now waiting for the daughter to die . . .

"You children, at any rate, will miss me, I know. Who will you write to twice a week, my poor Minet-Chéri? But it won't be so bad for you, after all, you've left me and built a nest for yourself far from me. But what about your elder brother, when he has to pass in front of my little house on his way back from his rounds, and no longer finds his glass of red-currant syrup there and a rose to carry off between his teeth? Yes, yes, of course you love me, but you're a girl, a female creature of my own species, my rival. But in his heart I never had any rival. Is my hair all right? No, I won't wear a cap, only my Spanish lace kerchief; he'll be here in a minute. All that dingy crowd has kicked up the dust, it's hard to breathe.

"It's nearly midday, isn't it? If no one has held him up your brother must be less than two miles away by now. Let the cat in; she too knows that it's nearly twelve o'clock. Every day, after her morning walk she comes back afraid of finding me well again. To sleep on my bed, night and day, what an earthly paradise for her! This morning, your brother had to go to Arnedon, Coulefeuilles and then home by Saint-André. I never forget his rounds. I follow him, you see. At Arnedon he's attending the small son of the fair Arthémise. Those love-children always suffer because their mothers have crushed them under their stays trying to hide them, the more's the pity. Yet after all, a lovely unrepentant creature, big with child, is not such an outrageous sight.

"Listen—listen! There's the trap at the top of the hill! Minet-Chéri, don't tell your brother that I had three attacks in the night. In the first place, because I forbid you to. And if you don't tell him I'll give you the bracelet with the three turquoises. Now I want none of your reasons—they bore me. It's nothing whatever to do with honesty. To begin with, in any case, I know better than you do what honesty is. But at my age there's only one virtue: not to make people unhappy. Quick now, put the second pillow behind my back so that I shall be sitting up when he comes in. And the two roses there, in the glass. It doesn't smell like a stuffy old woman in here, does it? Am I flushed? He'll think I'm not so well as I was yesterday, I know I ought not to have talked so much. Close the shutter a little, and then be a dear, Minet-Chéri, and lend me your powder-puff."

MY MOTHER AND THE FORBIDDEN FRUIT

THE time came when all her strength left her. She was amazed beyond measure and would not believe it. Whenever I arrived from Paris to see her, as soon as we were alone in the afternoon in her little house, she had always some sin to confess to me. On one occasion she turned up the hem of her dress, rolled her stocking down over her shin and displayed a purple bruise, the skin nearly broken.

"Just look at that!"

"What on earth have you done to yourself this time, mother?"

She opened wide eyes, full of innocence and embarrassment.

"You wouldn't believe it, but I fell downstairs!"

"How do you mean—'fell'?"

"Just what I said. I fell, for no reason. I was going downstairs and I fell. I can't understand it."

"Were you going down too quickly?"

"Too quickly? What do you call too quickly? I was going down quickly. Have I time to go downstairs majestically like the Sun King? And if that were all . . . But look at this!"

On her pretty arm, still so young above the faded hand, was a scald forming a large blister.

"Oh goodness! Whatever's that!"

"My foot-warmer."

"The old copper foot-warmer? The one that holds five quarts?"

"That's the one. Can I trust anything, when that foot-warmer has known me for forty years? I can't imagine what possessed it, it was boiling fast, I went to take it off the fire, and crack, something gave in my wrist. I was lucky to get nothing worse than that blister. But what a thing to happen! After that I let the cupboard alone. . . ."

She broke off, blushing furiously.

"What cupboard?" I demanded severely.

My mother fenced, tossing her head as though I were trying to put her on a lead.

"Oh, nothing! No cupboard at all!"

"Mother! I shall get cross!"

"Since I've said 'I let the cupboard alone,' can't you do the same for my sake? The cupboard hasn't moved from its place, has it? So, shut up about it!"

The cupboard was a massive object of old walnut, almost as broad as it was high, with no carving save the circular hole made by a Prussian bullet that had entered by the right-hand door and passed out through the back panel.

"Do you want it moved from the landing, mother?"

An expression like that of a young she-cat, false and glittery, appeared on her wrinkled face.

"I? No, it seems to me all right there—let it stay where it is!"

All the same, my doctor brother and I agreed that we must be on the watch. He saw my mother every day, since she had followed him and lived in the same village, and he looked after her with a passionate devotion which he hid. She fought against all her ills with amazing elasticity, forgot them, baffled them, inflicted on them signal if temporary defeats, recovered, during entire days, her vanished strength; and the sound of her battles, whenever I spent a few days with her, could be heard all over the house till I was irresistibly reminded of a terrier tackling a rat.

At five o'clock in the morning I would be awakened by the clank of a full bucket being set down in the kitchen sink immediately opposite my room.

"What are you doing with that bucket, mother? Couldn't you wait until Josephine arrives?"

And out I hurried. But the fire was already blazing, fed with dry wood. The milk was boiling on the blue-tiled charcoal stove. Nearby, a bar of chocolate was melting in a little water for my breakfast, and, seated squarely in her cane armchair, my mother was grinding the fragrant coffee which she roasted herself. The morning hours were always kind to her. She wore their rosy colours in her cheeks. Flushed with a brief return to health, she would gaze at the rising sun, while the church bell rang for early Mass, and rejoice at having tasted, while we still slept, so many forbidden fruits.

The forbidden fruits were the over-heavy bucket drawn up from the well, the firewood split with a bill-hook on an oaken block, the spade, the mattock, and above all the double steps propped against the gable-window of the wood-house. They were the climbing vine whose shoots she trained up to the gable-windows of the attic, the flowery spikes of the too-tall lilacs, the dizzy cat that had to be rescued from the ridge of the roof. All the accomplices of her old existence as a plump and sturdy little woman, all the minor rustic divinities who once obeyed her and made her so proud of doing without servants, now assumed the appearance and posi-tion of adversaries. But they reckoned without that love of combat which my mother was to keep till the end of her life. At seventy-one dawn still found her undaunted, if not always undamaged. Burnt by the fire, cut with the pruning knife, soaked by melting snow or spilt water, she had

always managed to enjoy her best moments of independ-
ence before the earliest risers had opened their shutters.
She was able to tell us of the cats' awakening, of what
was going on in the nests, of news gleaned, together with
the morning's milk and the warm loaf, from the milk-
maid and the baker's girl, the record in fact of the birth
of a new day.

It was not until one morning when I found the kitchen
unwarmed and the blue enamel saucepan hanging on the
wall, that I felt my mother's end to be near. Her illness
knew many respites, during which the fire flared up again
on the hearth, and the smell of fresh bread and melting
chocolate stole under the door together with the cat's
impatient paw. These respites were periods of unexpected
alarms. My mother and the big walnut cupboard were
discovered together in a heap at the foot of the stairs,
she having determined to transport it in secret from the
upper landing to the ground floor. Whereupon my elder
brother insisted that my mother should keep still and that
an old servant should sleep in the little house. But how
could an old servant prevail against a vital energy so
youthful and mischievous that it contrived to tempt and
lead astray a body already half fettered by death? My
brother, returning before sunrise from attending a distant
patient, one day caught my mother red-handed in the
most wanton of crimes. Dressed in her nightgown, but
wearing heavy gardening sabots, her little grey septuagen-
arian's plait of hair turning up like a scorpion's tail on
the nape of her neck, one foot firmly planted on the
crosspiece of the beech trestle, her back bent in the attitude
of the expert jobber, my mother, rejuvenated by an
indescribable expression of guilty enjoyment, in defiance
of all her promises and of the freezing morning dew, was
sawing logs in her own yard.

BYGONE SPRING

THE beak of a secateur goes clicking all down the rose-bordered paths. Another clicks in answer from the orchard. Presently the soil in the rose garden will be strewn with tender shoots, dawn-red at the tips, but green and juicy at the base. In the orchard the stiff, severed twigs of the apricot trees will keep their little flames of flower alight for another hour before they die, and the bees will see to it that none of them is wasted.

The hillside is dotted with white plum-trees like puffs of smoke, each of them filmy and dappled as a round cloud. At half-past five in the morning, under the dew and the slanting rays of sunrise, the young wheat is incontestably blue, the earth rust-red and the white plum-trees coppery pink. It is only for a moment, a magic delusion of light that fades with the first hour of day. Everything grows with miraculous speed. Even the tiniest plant thrusts upwards with all its strength. The peony, in the flush of its first month's growth, shoots up at such a pace that its scapes and scarcely unfolded leaves, pushing through the earth, carry with them the upper covering of it so that it hangs suspended like a roof burst asunder.

The peasants shake their heads: "April will bring us plenty of surprises." They bend wise brows over this folly, this annual imprudence of leaf and flower. They grow old, borne helplessly along in the wake of a terrible pupil who learns nothing from their experience. In the tilled valley, still criss-crossed with parallel rivulets, lines of green emerge above the inundation. Nothing can now delay the mole-like ascent of the asparagus, or extinguish the torch of the purple iris. The furious breaking of bonds infects birds, lizards and insects. Greenfinch, goldfinch, sparrow and chaffinch behave in the morning like farmyard fowl gorged with brandy-soaked grain. Ritual dances and mock battles, to the accompaniment of exaggerated cries, are renewed perpetually under our eyes, almost under our very hands. Flocks of birds and mating grey lizards share the same sun-warmed flag-stones, and when the children, wild with excitement, run aimlessly hither and thither, clouds of mayfly rise and hover round their heads.

Everything rushes onward, and I stay where I am. Do I not already feel more pleasure in comparing this spring with others that are past than in welcoming it? The torpor is blissful enough, but too aware of its own weight. And though my ecstasy is genuine and spon-taneous, it no longer finds expression. "Oh, look at those yellow cowslips! And the soapwort! And the unicorn tips of the lords and ladies are showing! . . ." But the cowslip, that wild primula, is a humble flower, and how can the uncertain mauve of the watery soapwort compare with a glowing peach tree? Its value for me lies in the stream that watered it between my tenth and fifteenth years. The slender cowslip, all stalk and rudi-mentary in blossom, still clings by a frail root to the meadow where I used to gather hundreds to straddle them along a string and then tie them into round balls, cool projectiles that struck the cheek like a rough, wet kiss.

I take good care nowadays not to pick cowslips and crush them into a greenish ball. I know the risk I should run if I did. Poor rustic enchantment, almost evaporated now, I cannot even bequeath you to another me: "Look Bel-Gazou, like this and then like that; first you straddle them on the string and then you draw it tight." "Yes, I see," says Bel-Gazou, "But it doesn't bounce; I'd rather have my indiarubber ball."

The secateurs click their beaks in the gardens. Shut me into a dark room and that sound will still bring in to me April sunshine, stinging the skin and treacherous as wine without a bouquet. With it comes the bee-scent of the pruned apricot trees, and a certain anguish, the un-easiness of one of those slight pre-adolescence indisposi-tions that develop, hang about for a time, improve, are cured one morning and reappear at night. I was ten or eleven years old but, in the company of my foster-mother who had become our cook, I still indulged in nursling whims. A grown girl in the dining-room, I would run to the kitchen to lick the vinegar off the salad leaves on the plate of Mélie, my faithful watch-dog, my fair-haired, fair-skinned slave. One April morning I called out to her, "Come along, Mélie, let's go and pick up the clippings from the apricot trees, Milien's at the espaliers."

She followed me, and the young housemaid, well-named Marie-la-Rose, came too, though I had not invited her. Milien, the day labourer, a handsome, crafty youth, was finishing his job, silently and without haste.

"Mélie, hold out your apron and let me put the clippings in it."

I was on my knees collecting the shoots starred with blossom. As though in play, Mélie went "Houl" at me and, flinging her apron over my head, folded me up in it and rolled me gently over. I laughed, thoroughly enjoy-ing making myself small and silly. But I began to stifle and came out from under it so suddenly that Milien and Marie-la-Rose, in the act of kissing, had not time to spring apart, nor Mélie to hide her guilty face.

Click of the secateur, harsh chatter of hard-billed birds! They tell of blossoming, of early sunshine, of sunburn on the forehead, of chilly shade, of uncomprehended repulsion, of childish trust betrayed, of suspicion, and of brooding sadness.

THE SEMPSTRESS

"Do you mean to say your daughter is nine years old," said a friend, "and she doesn't know how to sew? She really must learn to sew. In bad weather sewing is a better occupation for a child of that age than reading story books."

"Nine years old? And she can't sew?" said another friend. "When she was eight, my daughter embroidered this tray cloth for me, look at it. . . . Oh! I don't say it's fine needlework, but it's nicely done all the same. Nowadays my daughter cuts out her own underclothes. I can't bear anyone in my house to mend holes with pins!"

I meekly poured all this domestic wisdom over Bel-Gazou.

"You're nine years old and you don't know how to sew? You really must learn to sew . . ."

Flouting truth, I even added:

"When I was eight years old, I remember I embroidered a tray cloth. . . . Oh! It wasn't fine needlework, I dare say . . . And then, in bad weather . . ."

She has therefore learned to sew. And although—with one bare sunburnt leg tucked beneath her, and her body at ease in its bathing suit—she looks more like a fisher-boy mending a net than an industrious little girl, she seems to experience no boyish repugnance. Her hands, stained the colour of tobacco-juice by sun and sea, hem in a way that seems against nature; their version of the simple running stitch resembles the zigzag dotted lines of a road map, but she buttonholes and scallops with elegance and is severely critical of the embroidery of others.

She sews and kindly keeps me company if rain blurs the horizon of the sea. She also sews during the torrid hour when the spindle bushes gather their circles of shadow directly under them. Moreover, it sometimes happens that a quarter of an hour before dinner, black in her white dress—"Bel-Gazou! your hands and frock are clean, and don't forget it!"—she sits solemnly down with a square of material between her fingers. Then my friends applaud: "Just look at her! Isn't she good? That's right! Your mother must be pleased!"

Her mother says nothing—great joys must be controlled. But ought one to feign them? I shall speak the truth: I don't much like my daughter sewing.

When she reads, she returns all bewildered and with flaming cheeks, from the island where the chest full of precious stones is hidden, from the dismal castle where a fair-haired orphan child is persecuted. She is soaking up a tested and time-honoured poison, whose effects have long been familiar. If she draws, or colours pictures, a semi-articulate song issues from her, unceasing as the hum of bees round the privet. It is the same as the buzzing of flies as they work, the slow waltz of the house-painter, the refrain of the spinner at her wheel. But Bel-Gazou is silent when she sews, silent for hours on end, with her mouth firmly closed, concealing her large, new-cut incisors that bite into the moist heart of a fruit like little saw-edged blades. She is silent, and she—why not write down the word that frightens me—she is thinking.

A new evil? A torment that I had not foreseen? Sitting in a grassy dell, or half buried in hot sand and gazing out to sea, she is thinking, as well I know. She thinks rapidly when she is listening, with a well-bred pretence of discretion, to remarks imprudently exchanged above her head. But it would seem that with this needle-play she has discovered the perfect means of adventuring, stitch by stitch, point by point, along a road of risks and temptations. Silence . . . the hand armed with the steel dart moves back and forth. Nothing will stop the unchecked little explorer. At what moment must I utter the "Halt!" that will brutally arrest her in full flight? Oh, for those young embroiderers of bygone days, sitting on a hard little stool in the shelter of their mother's ample skirts! Maternal authority kept them there for years and years, never rising except to change the skein of silk, or to elope with a stranger. Think of Philomène de Watteville and her canvas on which she embroidered the loss and the despair of Albert Savarus. . . .

"What are you thinking about, Bel-Gazou?"

"Nothing, mother. I'm counting my stitches."

Silence. The needle pierces the material. A coarse trail of chain-stitch follows very unevenly in its wake. Silence. . . .

"Mother?"

"Darling?"

"Is it only when people are married that a man can put his arm round a lady's waist?"

"Yes. . . . No. . . . It depends. If they are very good friends and have known each other a long time, you understand . . . As I said before: it depends. Why do you want to know?"

"For no particular reason, mother."

Two stitches, ten misshapen chain-stitches.

"Mother? Is Madame X married?"

"She has been. She is divorced."

"I see. And Monsieur F, is he married?"

"Why, of course he is; you know that."

"Oh! Yes. . . . Then it's all right if one of the two is married?"

"What is all right?"

"To depend."

"One doesn't say: 'To depend.' "

"But you said just now that it depended."

"But what has it got to do with you? Is it any concern of yours?"

"No, mother."

I let it drop. I feel inadequate, self-conscious, displeased with myself. I should have answered differently and I could not think what to say.

Bel-Gazou also drops the subject; she sews. But she pays little attention to her sewing, overlaying it with pictures, associations of names and people, all the results of patient observation. A little later will come other curiosities, other questions, and especially other silences. Would to God that Bel-Gazou were the bewildered and simple child who questions crudely, open-eyed! But she is too near the truth, and too natural not to know as a birthright, that all nature hesitates before that most majestic and most disturbing of instincts, and that it is wise to tremble, to be silent and to lie when one draws near to it.

THE HOLLOW NUT

THREE shells like flower petals, white, nacreous, and transparent as the rosy snow that flutters down from the apple trees; two limpets, like Tonkinese hats with converging black rays on a yellow ground; something that looks like a lumpy, cartilaginous potato, inanimate but concealing a mysterious force that squirts, when it is squeezed, a crystal jet of salt water; a broken knife, a stump of pencil, a ring of blue beads and a book of transfers soaked by the sea; a small pink handkerchief, very dirty. . . . That is all. Bel-Gazou has completed the inventory of her left-hand pocket. She admires the mother-of-pearl petals, then drops them and crushes them under her espadrille. The hydraulic potato, the limpets and the transfers earn no better fate. Bel-Gazou retains only the knife, the pencil and the string of beads, all of which, like the handkerchief, are in constant use.

Her right-hand pocket contains fragments of that pinkish limestone that her parents, heaven knows why, name lithotamnium, when it is so simple to call it coral. "But it isn't coral, Bel-Gazou." Not coral? What do they know about it, poor wretches? Fragments, then, of lithotamnium, and a hollow nut, with a hole bored in it by the emerging maggot. There isn't a single nut-tree within three miles along the coast. The hollow nut, found on the beach, came there on the crest of a wave, from where? "From the other side of the world," affirms Bel-Gazou. "And it's very ancient, you know. You can see that by its rare wood. It's a rose-wood nut, like mother's little desk."

With the nut glued to her ear, she listens. "It sings. It says: 'Hu-u-u . . .' "

She listens, her mouth slightly open, her lifted eyebrows touching her fringe of straight hair. Standing thus motionless, and as though alienated by her preoccupation, she seems almost ageless. She stares at the familiar horizon of her holidays without seeing it. From the ruins of a thatched hut, deserted by the customs officer, Bel-Gazou's view embraces, on her right hand the Pointe-du-Nez, yellow with lichens, streaked with the bluish purple of a belt of mussels which the low tide leaves exposed; in the centre a wedge of sea, blue as new steel, thrust like an axe-head into the coast. On the left, an untidy privet hedge in full bloom, whose over-sweet almond scent fills the air, while the frenzied little feet of the bees destroy its flowers. The dry sea-meadow runs up as far as the hut and its slope hides the shore where her parents and friends lie limply baking on the sand. Presently, the entire family will enquire of Bel-Gazou: "But where were you? Why didn't you come down to the shore?" Bel-Gazou cannot understand this bay mania. Why the shore, always the shore, and nothing but the shore? The hut is just as interesting as that insipid sand, and there is the damp spinney, and the soapy water of the wash-house, and the field of lucerne as well as the shade of the fig tree. Grown up people are so constituted that one might spend a lifetime explaining to them—and all to no purpose. So it is with the hollow nut: "What's the use of that old nut?" Wiser far to hold one's tongue, and to hide, sometimes in a pocket, and sometimes in an empty vase or knotted in a handkerchief, the nut that a moment, impossible to foresee, will divest of all its virtue, but which meanwhile sings in Bel-Gazou's ear the song that holds her motionless as though she had taken root.

"I can see it! I can see the song! It's as thin as a hair, as thin as a blade of grass!"

Next year, Bel-Gazou will be past nine years old. She will have ceased to proclaim those inspired truths that confound her pedagogues. Each day carries her farther from that first stage of her life, so full, so wise, so perpetually mistrustful, so loftily disdainful of experience, of good advice, and humdrum wisdom. Next year, she will come back to the sands that gild her, to the salt butter and the foaming cider. She will find again her dilapidated hut, and her cityfied feet will once more acquire their natural horny soles, slowly toughened on the flints and ridges of the rough ground. But she may well fail to find again her childish subtlety and the keenness of her senses that can taste a scent, feel a colour and see,—"thin as a hair, thin as a blade of grass"—the cadence of an imaginary song.

SIDO

Translated by
Enid McLeod

CONTENTS

I

SIDO

"Leave my village? Why ever should I? You mustn't expect that. It's obvious you're as proud as can be, my poor Minet-Chéri, because you've been living in Paris since your marriage. It always makes me laugh to see how proud of living in Paris all Parisians are; the real ones seem to think the mere fact ennobles them and the others imagine they've gone up in the world. By that reckoning I could boast that my mother was born in the Boulevard Bonne-Nouvelle! As for you, you give your-self airs just because you've married a Parisian. A Parisian, did I call him? Your true-born Parisians haven't so much character in their faces. You might say that Paris de-faces them!"

She broke off and raised the net curtain that covered the window: "There goes Mademoiselle Thévenin triumph-antly parading her cousin from Paris all round the village. No need for her to say where Mistress Quériot comes from, with all that bosom, those tiny feet, ankles too slim for the weight of her body, two or three chains round her neck and that wonderfully dressed hair. I could tell with less than that that Mistress Quériot is a cashier in a big café. A Parisian cashier never bothers about anything except her head and her bust; the rest never sees daylight. And besides she doesn't walk enough and so her stomach gets fat. You'll see lots of that type of trunk-woman in Paris."

That was the way my mother used to talk in the days when I myself was a very young woman. But long before my marriage she had begun to set the provinces above Paris. From childhood I could remember judgments, excommunicatious as a rule, which she would bring out with a very special ring in her voice. Where did she find their pith and authority, she who never left her own province as much as three times a year? And whence came her gifts of acute perception and description, and that power of trenchant observation?

Even if I had not inherited it from her, she would, I think, have given me a love for the provinces, if by province one understands not merely a place or a region distant from the capital, but a strong sense of the social hierarchy, of the necessity for irreproachable conduct, and pride at inhabiting an ancient and honoured dwelling, closed on all sides but capable of opening at any moment on to its lofty barns, its well-filled hayloft, and its masters apt for the uses and the dignity of their house.

Like a true provincial, my charming mother, "Sido", often fixed her spiritual gaze on Paris. She was no stranger to its theatres, its fashions and its festivities, and by no means indifferent to them. But her love for these things was at its best a slightly aggressive passion, liable to coquetry and fits of the sulks, and revealing itself in strategic approaches and war dances. The little taste of Paris which she enjoyed every two years or so gave her enough to go on for all the rest of the time. She would return home laden with bar-chocolate, exotic foods and remnants of material, but above all with violet essence and theatre programmes, and at once start describing Paris to us. All its attractions were within her compass, since there was nothing she despised.

In a week she had visited the recently unearthed mummy, the museum extension and the new department store. She had heard the latest tenor and attended the lecture on *Burmese Music*. She brought back an inexpensive coat, serviceable stockings and very dear gloves. But best of all she brought back to us the darting glance of her grey eyes, and her rosy complexion that reddened when she was tired. She would arrive with fluttering wings, full of anxiety for everything which, deprived of her, was wont to lose its warmth and its zest for life. She never knew that, each time she came home, the smell of her grey squirrel pelisse, impregnated with her own blonde scent, chaste and feminine and far removed from all base, bodily seductions, bereft me of speech and almost of sense.

With a look and a gesture, she picked up all the threads again. How quick she was with her hands as she cut the pink paper-tape, unwrapped the colonial provisions, and carefully folded up again the black tarred paper that smelt of melted pitch. And as she talked she would call the cat, note out of the corner of her eye that my father had grown thinner, and touch and sniff my long plaits to make sure I had brushed my hair. Once when she was untying a piece of sibilant gilt twine, she noticed that, on the geranium imprisoned between the net curtain and one of the windows, a branch was hanging down, broken but still alive. She immediately set the broken branch, supporting it with a little cardboard splint, and bound it round twenty times with the gold string that she had unwound only a moment before. I shivered, and thought it was with jealousy; but it was merely a poetic echo awakened in me by the magic of that effectual aid sealed with gold.

She would have been a typical provincial if she had not entirely lacked a carping spirit. Critical she was, but her critical sense was sturdy, changeable, warm, and gay as a young lizard. She would pounce on the significant characteristic or blemish the moment it raised its head,

suddenly bring to light hidden beauties, and blaze a
shining trail through narrow minds.

"I've gone red, haven't I?" she would ask, as she
emerged from an encounter with one of those souls that
are like a dark passage. And indeed she was red. All
genuine Pythonesses, after plunging to the bottom of
another's being, come up again half-suffocated. Sometimes a perfectly ordinary visit left her crimson in the
face and exhausted, in the depths of the big armchair
with its cover of padded green rep.

"Oh those Vivenets! I'm absolutely worn out! My
goodness, those Vivenets!"

"What have they done to you, Mother?"

I had just returned from school and was making little
crescents with my teeth all over a crusty end of new bread
spread thick with butter and raspberry jelly.

"What have they done to me? They've been here.
What else—and what worse—could they have done to me?
Those two young newly-weds, accompanied by old
Madame Vivenet, came to pay a wedding visit. Oh those
Vivenets!"

She said little more about it to me, but later, when my
father came in, I heard the rest.

"Think of it," my mother remarked, "people who've
only been married four days! How unseemly! People
who've only been married four days should remain in
seclusion and not stroll about out of doors, or flaunt
themselves in society, or go about with the bride's or
the bridegroom's mother. Are you laughing? You've
no feeling for these things. Just to have seen that four
days' old bride still makes me red all over. I'll do her the
credit to say that she, at least, was embarrassed. She
looked as though she'd lost her petticoat or sat on a
newly-painted bench. But the man is a horror! He's

got strangler's thumbs and a pair of gimlet eyes lurking
in the depths of his two ordinary ones. He's one of those
men who have a memory for figures, and lay their hands
on their hearts when they're telling lies, and feel thirsty
in the afternoons—always a sign of a sour stomach and an
irritable disposition."

"Bravo!" applauded my father.

Soon it was my turn, for having begged to be allowed
to wear socks in summer. "When will you leave off wanting to imitate Mimi Antonin in everything she does,
whenever she comes to spend the holidays with her
grandmother? Mimi Antonin belongs to Paris and you
belong here. If the Parisian children want to show their
bare shanks in summer, and go about in winter in such
short drawers that you can see their poor little red
bottoms, let them. The one idea of Parisian mothers,
when their children shiver, is to give them a little tippet
of white goat fur. In really bitter cold they add a little
cap to match. Besides, you can't begin wearing socks
when you're eleven, specially with the calves I've given
you. You'd look like a tight-rope dancer and the only
thing lacking would be a tin begging-bowl."

That was the way she used to talk, never hesitating for a
word and never laying down what I called her weapons:
in other words two pairs of glasses, a pocket knife, often
a clothes brush, a pair of secateurs, some old gloves, and
sometimes that cane sceptre splaying out into a sort of
three-lobed tennis racquet, which is known as a carpet-
beater and used for beating curtains and upholstery.
The only ritual dates which my mother's caprice would
consent to observe were those which they celebrate in the
provinces with drastic cleanings and launderings and the
storing of furs and woollens. But she took no pleasure
in the bottom of cupboards, nor in the funereal odour of

camphor-powder, which in any case she never used,
preferring a few cigars cut into sections that looked like
caramels, the dottles of my father's meerschaum pipes,
and fat spiders which she would shut into the cupboard
that was the hunting-ground of the silvery clothes-moths.

The fact is that, though she was active and always on
the go, she was not a sedulous housewife. She was clean
and tidy, fastidious even, but without a trace of that
solitary, maniacal spirit that counts napkins, lumps of
sugar, and full bottles. With a flannel in her hands, and
one eye on the servant dawdling over her window-clean-
ing and smiling at the man next door, she would utter
nervous exclamations like impatient cries for freedom.

"When I take a lot of time and trouble wiping my
Chinese cups," she would say, "I can actually feel myself
getting older."

But she always persevered loyally until the job was
finished. Then off she would go, down the two steps that
led into the garden, and at once her resentment and her
nervous exasperation subsided. The presence of plants
always acted on her like a restorative, and she had a
curious way of lifting roses by the chin to look them full
in the face.

"Don't you think that pansy looks just like Henry VIII
of England with his round beard?" she said once. "Yellow
and purple pansies have such crafty faces, I don't really
care for them much."

In my home village there were hardly twenty houses
without a garden. The worst off enjoyed a backyard,
whether or not it was cultivated or roofed with a vine
trellis. Each frontage hid a long back garden, joined to the
others by a party wall. These back gardens gave the

village its character. There we all lived in summer, and there the washing was done; in winter the wood was chopped there; and all the year round it was the place for odd jobs, while the children played under the cart-sheds and perched on the side-rails of the empty hay-wains.

The enclosures adjoining our own had no particular mystery about them, but in ours both the "upper garden" and the "lower garden" were shielded by the slope of the ground, the high and ancient walls, and screens of trees. The reverberating hill-side echoed all noises, carrying news from the little island of kitchen-gardens surrounded by houses as far as our "public park".

From our garden, to the South we could hear Miton sneezing as he dug, and talking to his white dog. Every Fourteenth of July he used to dye its head blue and its hindquarters red. To the North there was old Mother Adolphe singing a little hymn as she tied up bunches of violets for the altar of our church, which had lost its belfry when it was struck by lightning. To the East, a sad little tinkle announced that a client had called to see the lawyer. Let no one talk to me of provincial suspiciousness. Suspiciousness indeed! Our gardens told each other everything.

How pleasant it was, that civilised life in our gardens, with its exchanges of courtesies and amenities between the kitchen-garden and the "floral", the shrubbery and the poultry-yard! What harm ever came over an espalier trained along a party-wall whose coping-stones, held together with lichen and glowing yellow stonecrop, served as a promenade for toms and she-cats? On the other side, where the houses gave on the street, cheeky children mooned about, playing marbles and tucking up their petticoats when they played in the stream; neighbours eyed each other and flung little curses, a laugh or a bit of peel in the wake of each passer-by, while the men lounged in their doorways smoking and spitting. From our own façade, iron-grey with tall, faded shutters, no sound emerged but that of my fumbling scales, the barking of a dog when the bell rang, and the song of the green canaries in their cage.

Perhaps our neighbours tried to emulate in their gardens the peace of ours, where the children never fought and where beasts and men lived their lives tranquilly together; a garden where for the space of thirty years a husband and wife dwelt with never a harsh word between them.

In those days there were bitter winters and burning summers. Since then I have known summers which, when I close my eyes, are the colour of ochre-yellow earth, cracking between stalks of corn; and beneath the giant umbels of wild parsnip, the blue or grey of the sea. But no summer, save those of my childhood, enshrines the memory of scarlet geraniums and the glowing spikes of foxgloves. No winter now is ever pure white beneath a sky charged with slate-coloured clouds foretelling a storm of thicker snowflakes yet to come, and thereafter a thaw glittering with a thousand water-drops and bright with spear-shaped buds. How that sky used to lower over the snow-laden roof of the haylofts, the weathercock, and the bare boughs of the walnut-tree, making the she-cats flatten their ears! The quiet vertical fall of the snow became oblique and, as I wandered about the garden catching its flying flakes in my mouth, a faint booming as of a distant sea arose above my hooded head. Warned by her antennæ, my mother would come out on the terrace, sample the weather and call out to me:

"A gale from the West! Run and shut the skylights in the

barn! And the door of the coach-house! And the window of the back room!"

Eager cabin-boy of the family vessel, I would rush off, my sabots clattering, thrilled if, from the depths of that hissing turmoil of white and blue-black, a flash of lightning and a brief mutter of thunder, children of February and the West wind, together filled one of the abysses of the sky. I would try then to shudder and believe that the end of the world had come.

But when the din was at its height, there would be my mother, peering through a big brass-rimmed magnifying-glass, lost in wonder as she counted the branched crystals of a handful of snow she had just snatched from the very jaws of the West wind as it flung itself upon our garden.

It was the reflected glow of your blazing line along the terrace, O geraniums, and yours, O foxgloves, springing up amidst the coppice, that gave my childish cheeks their rosy warmth. For Sido loved red and pink in the garden, the burning shades of roses, lychnis, hydrangeas and red-hot pokers. She even loved the winter-cherry, although she declared that its pulpy pink flowers, veined with red, reminded her of the lights of a freshly killed calf. She made a reluctant pact with the East wind. "I know how to get on with him," she would say. But she remained suspicious and, out of all the cardinal and collateral points of the compass, it was on that icy treacherous point, with its murderous pranks, that she kept her eye. But she trusted him with lily of the valley bulbs, some begonias, and mauve autumn crocuses, those dim lanterns of cold twilights.

Except for one mound with a clump of cherry-laurels

overshadowed by a maiden-hair tree—whose skate-shaped leaves I used to give to my school friends to press between the pages of their atlases—the whole warm garden basked in a yellow light that shimmered into red and violet; but whether this red and violet sprang then, and still spring, from feelings of happiness or from dazzled sight, I could not tell. Those were summers when the heat quivered up from the hot yellow gravel and pierced the plaited rushes of my wide-brimmed hats, summers almost without nights. For even then I so loved the dawn that my mother granted it to me as a reward. She used to agree to wake me at half-past three and off I would go, an empty basket on each arm, towards the kitchen-gardens that sheltered in the narrow bend of the river, in search of strawberries, black-currants, and hairy gooseberries.

At half-past three everything slumbered still in a primal blue, blurred and dewy, and as I went down the sandy road the mist, grounded by its own weight, bathed first my legs, then my well-built little body, reaching at last to my mouth and ears, and finally to that most sensitive part of all, my nostrils. I went alone, for there were no dangers in that free-thinking countryside. It was on that road and at that hour that I first became aware of my own self, experienced an inexpressible state of grace, and felt one with the first breath of air that stirred, the first bird, and the sun so newly born that it still looked not quite round.

"Beauty" my mother would call me, and "Jewel-of-pure-gold"; then she would let me go, watching her creation—her masterpiece, as she said—grow smaller as I ran down the slope. I may have been pretty; my mother and the pictures of me at that period do not always agree. But what made me pretty at that moment was my youth and the dawn, my blue eyes deepened by the greenery all round me, my fair locks that would only be brushed smooth on my return, and my pride at being awake when other children were asleep.

I came back when the bell rang for the first Mass. But not before I had eaten my fill, not before I had described a great circle in the woods, like a dog out hunting on its own, and tasted the water of the two hidden springs which I worshipped. One of them bubbled out of the ground with a crystalline spurt and a sort of sob, and then carved its own sandy bed. But it was no sooner born than it lost confidence and plunged underground again. The other spring, almost invisible, brushed over the grass like a snake, and spread itself out secretly in the middle of a meadow where the narcissus, flowering in a ring, alone bore witness to its presence. The first spring tasted of oak-leaves, the second of iron and hyacinth stalks. The mere mention of them makes me hope that their savour may fill my mouth when my time comes, and that I may carry hence with me that imagined draught.

In her garden my mother had a habit of addressing to the four cardinal points not only direct remarks and replies that sounded, when heard from our sitting-room, like brief inspired soliloquies, but the actual manifestations of her courtesy, which generally took the form of plants and flowers. But in addition to these points—to Cèbe and the Rue des Vignes, to Mother Adolphe and Maître de Fourolles—there was also a zone of collateral points, more distant and less defined, whose contact with us was by means of stifled sounds and signals. My childish pride and imagination saw our house as the central point of a Mariner's Chart of gardens, winds and rays of light, no section of which lay quite beyond my mother's influence.

I could gain my liberty at any moment by means of an easy climb over a gate, a wall, or a little sloping roof, but as soon as I landed back on the gravel of our own garden, illusion and faith returned to me. For as soon as she had asked me: "Where have you come from?" and frowned the ritual frown, my mother would resume her placid, radiant garden-face, so much more beautiful than her anxious indoor-face. And merely because she held sway there and watched over it all, the walls grew higher, the enclosures which I had so easily traversed by jumping from wall to wall and branch to branch, became unknown lands, and I found myself once more among the familiar wonders.

"Is that you I hear, Cèbe?" my mother would call. "Have you seen my cat?"

She pushed back her wide-brimmed hat of burnt straw until it slid down her shoulders, held by a brown taffeta ribbon round her neck, and threw her head back to confront the sky with her fearless grey glance and her face the colour of an autumn apple. Did her voice strike the bird on the weathercock, the hovering honey-buzzard, the last leaf on the walnut-tree or the dormer window which, at the first light, swallowed up the barn owls? Then—though it was certain to happen, the surprise was never failing—from a cloud on the left the voice of a prophet with a bad cold would let fall a: "No, Madame Colê . . . ê . . . ttel" which seemed to be making its way with great difficulty through a curly beard and blankets of fog, and slithering over ponds vaporous with cold. Or perhaps: "Ye . . . es, Madame Colê . . . ê . . . ttel", the

voice of a shrill angel would sing on the right, probably
perched on the spindle-shaped cirrus cloud which was
sailing along to meet the young moon. "She's he . . . e . . .
ard you. She's go . . . oing through the li . . . i . . . lacs."

"Thank you!" called my mother at random. "If that's
you, Cèbe, just give me back my stake and my planting-
out line, will you! I need them to get my lettuces straight.
But be careful. I'm close to the hydrangeas!" As if it were
the offering of a dream, the prank of a 'witches' sabbath,
or an act of magical levitation, the stake, wound round
with ten yards of small cord, sailed through the air and
came to rest at my mother's feet.

On other occasions she would offer to lesser, invisible
spirits a tribute of flowers. Faithful to her ritual, she threw
back her head and scanned the sky: "Who wants some of
my double red violets?" she cried.

"I do, Madame Colê . . . ê . . . tte!" answered the
mysterious one to the East, in her plaintive, feminine
voice.

"Here you are, then!" and the little bunch, tied together
with a juicy jonquil leaf, flew through the air, to be
gratefully received by the plaintive Orient. "How lovely
they smell! To think I can't grow any as good!"

'Of course you can't,' I would think, and felt inclined
to add: 'It's all a question of the air they breathe.'

Always up at dawn and sometimes before day, my
mother attached particular importance to the cardinal
points of the compass, as much for the good as for the
harm they might bring. It is because of her and my deep-
rooted love for her that first thing every morning, and
while I am still snug in bed, I always ask: "Where is the

wind coming from?" only to be told in reply: "It's a lovely day," or "The Palais-Royal's full of sparrows," or "The weather's vile" or "seasonable". So nowadays I have to rely on myself for the answer, by watching which way a cloud is moving, listening for ocean rumblings in the chimney, and letting my skin enjoy the breath of the West wind, a breath as moist and vital and laden with portents as the twofold divergent snortings of some friendly monster. Or it may be that I shrink into myself with hatred before that fine-cold-dry enemy the East wind, and his cousin of the North. That was what my mother used to do, as she covered with paper cornets all the little plant creatures threatened by the russet moon. "It's going to freeze," she would say, "the cat's dancing."

Her hearing, which remained keen, kept her informed too, and she would intercept Æolian warnings.

"Listen over Moutiers!" she used to say, lifting her forefinger where she stood near the pump, between the hydrangeas and the group of rose bushes. That was her reception point for the information coming from the west over the lowest of the garden walls. "D'you hear? Take the garden chairs indoors, and your book and hat. It's raining over Moutiers; in two or three minutes more it'll be raining here."

I strained my ears "over Moutiers"; from the horizon came a steady sound of beads plopping into water and the flat smell of the rain-pitted pond as it sluiced up against its slimy green banks. And I would wait for a second or two, so that the gentle drops of a summer shower, falling on my cheeks and lips, might bear witness to the infallibility of her whom only one person in the world— my father—called "Sido".

Certain omens, dimmer since her death, haunt me still. One is concerned with the Zodiac, another is entirely botanical, and others again have to do with the winds, the phases of the moon, and subterranean waters. It was because those omens were only free to be effective and decisive in the wide air of our province that my mother found Paris irksome.

"I could live in Paris only if I had a beautiful garden," she would confess to me. "And even then! I can't imagine a Parisian garden where I could pick those big bearded oats I sew on a bit of cardboard for you because they make such sensitive barometers." I chide myself for having lost the very last of those rustic barometers made of oat grains whose two awns, as long as a shrimp's feelers, crucified on a card, would turn to the left or the right according to whether it was going to be fine or wet.

No one could equal Sido, either, at separating and counting the talc-like skins of onions. "One . . . two . . . three coats; three coats on the onions!" And letting her spectacles or her lorgnette fall on her lap, she would add pensively: "That means a hard winter. I must have the pump wrapped in straw. Besides, the tortoise has dug itself in already, and the squirrels round about Guille-mette have stolen quantities of walnuts and cob-nuts for their stores. Squirrels always know everything."

If the newspapers foretold a thaw my mother would shrug her shoulders and laugh scornfully. "A thaw? Those Paris meteorologists can't teach me anything about that! Look at the cat's paws!" Feeling chilly, the cat had indeed folded her paws out of sight beneath her, and shut her eyes tight. "When there's only going to be a short spell of cold," went on Sido, "the cat rolls herself into a turban with her nose against the root of her tail. But when it's going to be really bitter, she tucks in the pads of her front paws and rolls them up like a muff."

All the year round she kept racks full of plants in pots

standing on green-painted wooden steps. There were rare
geraniums, dwarf rose-bushes, spiræas with misty white
and pink plumes, a few "succulents", hairy and squat as
crabs, and murderous cacti. Two warm walls formed an
angle which kept the harsh winds from her trial-ground,
which consisted of some red earthenware bowls in which
I could see nothing but loose, dormant earth.

"Don't touch!"

"But nothing's coming up!"

"And what do you know about it? Is it for you to
decide? Read what's written on the labels stuck in the
pots! These are seeds of blue lupin; that's a narcissus bulb
from Holland; those are seeds of winter-cherry; that's a
cutting of hibiscus—no, of course it isn't a dead twig!
—and those are some seeds of sweet-peas whose flowers
have ears like little hares. And that . . . and that . . ."

"Yes, and that?"

My mother pushed her hat back, nibbled the chain of
her lorgnette, and put the problem frankly to me:

"I'm really very worried. I can't remember whether it
was a family of crocus bulbs I planted there, or the
chrysalis of an emperor moth."

"We've only got to scratch to find out."

A swift hand stopped mine. Why did no one ever
model or paint or carve that hand of Sido's, tanned and
wrinkled early by household tasks, gardening, cold
water and the sun, with its long, finely-tapering fingers
and its beautiful, convex, oval nails?

"Not on your life! If it's the chrysalis, it'll die as soon
as the air touches it, and if it's the crocus, the light will
shrivel its little white shoot and we'll have to begin all
over again. Are you taking in what I say? You won't
touch it?"

"No, mother."

As she spoke her face, alight with faith and an all-embracing curiosity, was hidden by another, older face, resigned and gentle. She knew that I should not be able to resist, any more than she could, the desire to know, and that like herself I should ferret in the earth of that flower-pot until it had given up its secret. I never thought of our resemblance, but she knew I was her own daughter and that, child though I was, I was already seeking for that sense of shock, the quickened heart-beat, and the sudden stoppage of the breath—symptoms of the private ecstasy of the treasure-seeker. A treasure is not merely something hidden under the earth, or the rocks, or the sea. The vision of gold and gems is but a blurred mirage. To me the important thing is to lay bare and bring to light something that no human eye before mine has gazed upon.

She knew then that I was going to scratch on the sly in her trial-ground until I came upon the upward-climbing claw of the cotyledon, the sturdy sprout urged out of its sheath by the spring. I thwarted the blind purpose of the bilious-looking, black-brown chrysalis, and hurled it from its temporary death into a final nothingness.

"You don't understand . . . you can't understand. You're nothing but a little eight-year-old murderess . . . or is it ten? You just can't understand something that wants to live." That was the only punishment I got for my misdeeds; but that was hard enough for me to bear.

Sido loathed flowers to be sacrificed. Although her one idea was to give, I have seen her refuse a request for flowers to adorn a hearse or a grave. She would harden her heart, frown, and answer "No" with a vindictive look.

"But it's for poor Monsieur Enfert who died last night! Poor Madame Enfert's so pathetic, she says if she could see her husband depart covered with flowers, it would console her! And you've got such lovely moss-roses, Madame Colette."

"My moss-roses on a corpse! What an outrage!"

It was an involuntary cry, but even after she had pulled herself together she still said: "No. My roses have not been condemned to die at the same time as Monsieur Enfert."

But she gladly sacrificed a very beautiful flower to a very small child, a child not yet able to speak, like the little boy whom a neighbour to the East proudly brought into the garden one day, to show him off to her. My mother found fault with the infant's swaddling clothes, for being too tight, untied his three-piece bonnet and his unnecessary woollen shawl, and then gazed to her heart's content on his bronze ringlets, his cheeks, and the enormous, stern black eyes of a ten months' old baby boy, really so much more beautiful than any other boy of ten months! She gave him a *cuisse-de-nymphe-émue* rose, and he accepted it with delight, put it in his mouth, and sucked it; then he kneaded it with his powerful little hands and tore off the petals, as curved and carmine as his own lips.

"Stop it, you naughty boy!" cried his young mother.

But mine, with looks and words, applauded his massacre of the rose, and in my jealousy I said nothing.

She also regularly refused to lend double geraniums, pelargoniums, lobelias, dwarf rose-bushes and spiræa for the wayside altars on Corpus Christi Day, for although she was baptised and married in church, she always held aloof from Catholic trivialities and pageantries. But she gave me permission, when I was between eleven and twelve, to attend catechism classes and to join in the hymns at the Evening Service.

On the first of May, with my comrades of the catechism class, I laid lilac, camomile and roses before the altar of the Virgin, and returned full of pride to show my "blessed posy". My mother laughed her irreverent laugh and, looking at my bunch of flowers, which was bringing the may-bugs into the sitting-room right under the lamp, she said: "D'you suppose it wasn't already blessed before?"

I do not know where she got her aloofness from any form of worship. I ought to have tried to find out. My biographers, who get little information from me, some- times depict her as a simple farmer's wife and sometimes make her out to be "whimsical Bohemian". One of them, to my astonishment, goes so far as to accuse her of having written short literary works for young persons!

In reality, this Frenchwoman spent her childhood in the Yonne, her adolescence among painters, journalists and musicians in Belgium, where her two elder brothers had settled, and then returned to the Yonne, where she married twice. But whence, or from whom, she got her sensitive understanding of country matters and her discriminating appreciation of the provinces I am unable to say. I sing her praises as best I may, and celebrate the native lucidity which, in her, dimmed and often ex- tinguished the lesser lights painfully lit through the contact of what she called "the common run of mankind".

I once saw her hang up a scarecrow in a cherry-tree to frighten the blackbirds, because our kindly neighbour of the West, who always had a cold and was shaken with bouts of sneezing, never failed to disguise his cherry- trees as old tramps, and crown his currant-bushes with battered opera-hats. A few days later I found my mother beneath the tree, motionless with excitement, her head turned towards the heavens in which she would allow human religions no place.

"Sssh! Look!"

A blackbird, with a green and violet sheen on his dark plumage, was pecking at the cherries, drinking their juice and lacerating their rosy pulp.

"How beautiful he is!" whispered my mother. "D'you see how he uses his claw? And the movements of his head, and that arrogance of his? See how he twists his beak to dig out the stone! And you notice that he only goes for the ripest ones."

"But, mother, the scarecrow!"

"Sssh! The scarecrow doesn't worry him!"

"But, mother, the cherries!"

My mother brought the glance of her rain-coloured eyes back to earth: "The cherries? Yes, of course, the cherries."

In those eyes there flickered a sort of wild gaiety, a contempt for the whole world, a light-hearted disdain which cheerfully spurned me along with everything else. It was only momentary, and it was not the first time I had seen it. Now that I know her better I can interpret those sudden gleams in her face. They were, I feel, kindled by an urge to escape from everyone and everything, to soar to some high place where only her own writ ran. If I am mistaken, leave me to my delusion.

But there, under the cherry-tree, she returned to earth once more among us, weighed down with anxieties, and love, and a husband and children who clung to her. Faced with the common round of life, she became good and comforting and humble again.

"Yes of course, the cherries . . . you must have cherries too."

The blackbird, gorged, had flown off, and the scarecrow waggled his empty opera-hat in the breeze.

"As sure as I'm here," she used to tell me, "I've seen it snowing in the month of July."

"In the month of July!"

"Yes, on a day like this."

"Like this. . . ."

I had a habit of repeating the ends of her sentences. My voice was already lower than hers, but I used to imitate her way of talking, and I still do.

"Yes, like this," said my mother, blowing away an airy wisp of silvery fluff, pulled from the coat of the Havanese bitch she was combing. The fluff, finer than spun glass, was caught gently up in a little stream of ascending air, rose to the ceiling and was lost to view in the dazzle of light there.

"It was a lovely day," went on my mother, "lovely and warm. All of a sudden the wind changed, caught the tail end of a storm and piled it all up, to the East of course. Next came a spatter of very cold, fine hail, and finally a heavy fall of big, thick snowflakes. Snow covered the roses and lay on the ripe cherries and the tomatoes. The red geraniums had had no time to cool down, and they melted the snow as fast as it covered them. All *his* tricks, of course," she concluded, with a jerk of her elbow and a defiant thrust of her chin, towards the lofty throne, the invisible Judgment Seat, of her enemy the East, whom I tried to see beyond the warm, white, tumbling clouds of a fine summer day.

"But I've seen something much stranger than that!" went on my mother.

"Stranger than that?"

Could it be that one day, on her way to Bel-Air or on the road to Thury, she had met the East in person?

Perhaps a huge foot, blue with cold, and the frozen pool of an immense eyeball, had cleft the clouds so that she might describe them to me?

"I was expecting your brother Léo at the time, and one day I was out driving the mare, in the victoria."

"The same mare we have now?"

"Why of course the same mare. You're only ten. D'you suppose one changes a mare as one does a chemise? In those days our mare was a beautiful creature, a bit on the young side, and sometimes I let Antoine drive her. But I always went in the victoria to reassure her."

I remember wanting to ask: "To reassure whom?" but I refrained, so that I could go on believing in the possible ambiguity: after all, why should not my mother's presence have reassured the victoria?

"You see, when she heard my voice she felt quieter."

Of course she did, very quiet and all spick and span, in her blue upholstery between her two handsome carriage-lamps with their brass crowns of cloverleaf pattern. The very image of a reassured victoria, couldn't be more so!

"My goodness, daughter, what a silly look you've got on your face at this moment! Are you listening to me?"

"Yes, mother."

"Well then, it was one of those terribly hot days, and we'd been for a long drive. I was enormous and I felt very heavy. We were on our way back at a walking pace, and I remember I'd been cutting flowering broom. We'd just drawn level with the cemetery—no, this isn't a ghost story—when a cloud, a real southern cloud, copper-coloured with a little rim of quicksilver all round it, began to climb rapidly up the sky, gave a clap of thunder and shot out water like a bucket with a hole in it. Down got Antoine and wanted to put up the hood to shelter me. But

I said to him: "No, the first thing is to hold the mare's
head, because if it hails, she'll bolt while you're putting
up the hood." So he held the mare who was dancing a
bit where she stood, and I started talking to her just as if it
had neither rained nor thundered, you know, just as if we
were going out for a quiet drive in fine weather. Meanwhile an unbelievable downpour of water was falling on
my wretched little sunshade. When the cloud had passed,
I was left sitting in a hip-bath, Antoine was wet through
and the hood full of water, and what was more, quite
warm water. And when Antoine went to empty the hood,
what do you think we found in it? Frogs, tiny live frogs,
at least thirty of them. They'd been carried through the
air, owing to some freak of the Southern atmosphere, by
one of those hot whirlwinds or tornadoes whose corkscrew foot picks up a tuft of sand and seeds and insects
and carries them a hundred leagues away. And that I've
seen with my own eyes!"

She brandished the steel comb we used for unravelling
the knots in the coats of the Havanese bitch and the
angoras, not in the least astonished that meteorological
marvels should have waited for her to pass that way, and
treated her so familiarly.

You can easily understand how the South wind,
conjured up by Sido, rose before my mind's eye, swirling
on its corkscrew foot rooted in the Libyan Desert, and
bedecked with seeds and sand and dead butterflies. It
shook its shapeless, dishevelled head and out fell water
and the rain of frogs. I can see it still.

"But what a stupid expression you've got to-day,
daughter! As a matter of fact you're much prettier when
you look stupid, it's a pity it happens so seldom. You've
already got the habit of expressing far more than the
occasion warrants, which is one of my failings. When I

mislay my thimble I always look as though I'd lost a
beloved relation. When you put on a stupid look, your
eyes get bigger and your mouth drops open and that
makes you look younger. What are you thinking about?"

"Nothing, mother."

"I don't believe you, but it's a very good imitation.
Really very good, daughter, you're a prodigy of sweetness
and insipidity!"

I would tremble and blush under her barbed praise, her
piercing look and her voice with its rising final inflexions,
so surely pitched. She never called me "daughter" except
to underline a criticism or a reproof. But both voice and
look were swift to change.

"O my Jewel-of-pure-gold, it isn't true, you're neither
stupid nor pretty, you're just my peerless little girl.
Where are you going?"

Absolution lent me wings, as it does to all mercurial
creatures, and having been duly kissed I was already
light-heartedly preparing for flight.

"Don't go far at this time of day. It will be sunset
in . . ." She consulted, not her watch, but the height of the
sun above the horizon, the tobacco flowers or the datura,
that drowse all day until the evening wakes them. " . . . in
half an hour, the white tobacco is smelling sweet already.
Would you like to take some monk's-hood and columbines and campanulas to Adrienne Saint-Aubin and give
her back the *Revue des Deux-Mondes?* Change your hair-
ribbon, put on a pale-blue one, your complexion's just
right for pale blue this evening."

I wore those wide ribbons tied round my head—"à la
Vigée-Lebrun" as my mother called it—until I was
twenty-two. And to tell me to change my ribbon and
take a message of flowers for her, was my mother's way of
letting me know that for the space of an hour or a day I

was looking particularly pretty, and that she felt proud of me. With the ribbon like an outspread butterfly above my forehead and some of my hair pulled forward on my temples, I took the flowers from Sido as she cut them.

"Now be off with you! Give the double columbines to Adrienne Saint-Aubin and the rest to anyone you like among the neighbours. Over to the East there's someone ill, Mother Adolphe. If you go to her house . . ."

Before she had time to finish her sentence I recoiled with a bound, jibbing like an animal before the smell and sight of illness. My mother hung on to me by the end of one of my plaits, and that sudden wild face of hers, free of all constraint, without charity or humanity, leapt out from behind her face of everyday, as she whispered: "Don't say it! I know, I'm just the same. But one mustn't say it, ever! Now be off with you. Did you put those front locks in curl-papers again last night, you minx? Oh well . . ."

She let go of my rein of hair and stood away from me so as to see me better: "Go and show them what I can produce!"

But in spite of her admonition, I did not go to see the sick woman to the East. I went down the street as though it were a ford, jumping from one cobbled stone to the next, and did not stop till I reached the house where lived my mother's strange friend, Adrienne.

I am sure that not even her own children and nephews can have kept a more vivid memory of her than I have. A lively creature, both alert and dreamy, with beautiful, yellow gipsy eyes beneath frizzy hair, she used to wander about in a sort of rustic rapture, as though daily impelled by some nomadic instinct. Her house resembled her in its untidiness and shared with her a grace denied to orderly places and people. In her garden, roses and wistaria clambered up the yew-trees to escape from the damp, funereal gloom of the smothering greenery, and had to use so much energy in their efforts to reach the sunlight, that their attenuated parent stems grew bare as reptiles. A thousand roses, taking refuge in the tree-tops, bloomed out of reach among the wistaria with its long, hanging falls, and the purple bignonia, which had routed the exhausted clematis.

Under this thatch of creepers, Adrienne's house was stifling during the hot weather. Certain of finding there piles of books all falling apart, mushrooms picked at dawn, wild strawberries, fossilised ammonites, and, when they were in season, grey Puisaye truffles, I would glide in like a cat. But any cat hesitates, non-plussed, before a super-cat. Adrienne's presence, her indifference, and that well-guarded secret which glittered in the depths of her yellow eyes, filled me with a vague uneasiness whose significance I daresay I apprehended. She made a kind of fierce art of disregarding me, and her all-embracing gipsy indifference wounded me as though it were for me alone.

Once when my mother and Adrienne were suckling their infants, a daughter and son respectively, they changed babes for fun. So occasionally Adrienne would laughingly challenge me with a: "You whom I once fed with my own milk!" At that I would blush so madly that my mother frowned and scanned my face to find out what could have made me so red. How was I to conceal from that clear gaze of hers, blade-grey and threatening, the image that tormented me, of Adrienne's swarthy breast and its hard, purple knob?

As I wandered about Adrienne's house, forgotten among the tottering piles of books—which included the complete set of the *Revue des Deux-Mondes*—, among the countless volumes of an old medical library that smelt like a cellar, among giant shells and half-dried medicinal herbs, bowls of cats' food gone sour, the dog Perdreau, and the black tom-cat with the white mask who was called Colette and ate plain chocolate, I would start at the sound of a call that came over the rose-fettered yews and the emaciated thuyas paralysed by the python coils of a wistaria. My mother had suddenly appeared at a window in our house, as though to give the alarm for fire or burglars, and was calling my name. What a strange thing is the sense of guilt in a blameless child! I rushed home at once, putting on a guileless expression and the breathlessness of one taken by surprise.

"All this time at Adrienne's?"

That was all she said, but what a tone of voice! Sido's acute perception and jealousy on the one hand, and my excessive confusion on the other, led, as I grew older, to a cooling of the friendship between the two women. They never had any altercation, and no explanation ever took place between my mother and me. What was there for us to explain? Adrienne was careful never to entice me or detain me. One can be captivated without love. And I was already ten or eleven years old. It took me a very long time to associate a disturbing memory, a certain warmth in the heart, and the enchanted transformation of a person and her dwelling, with the idea of a first seduction.

Sido and my childhood were both, and because of each other, happy at the centre of that imaginary star whose eight points bear the names of the cardinal and collateral points of the compass. My twelfth year saw the beginning of misfortune, of departures and separations. With so much to bear courageously every day in secret, my mother had less time for her garden and her last-born.

I would like to have illustrated these pages with a photograph of her. But I could only have been content with a Sido standing in her garden, between the hydrangeas, the weeping ash and the ancient walnut-tree. That was where I left her when the time came for me to take leave alike of happiness and my earliest youth. I did see her there once again, for a fleeting moment in the spring of 1928. And there I am sure she still is, with her head thrown back and her inspired look, summoning and gathering to her the sounds and whispers and omens that speed faithfully towards her down the eight paths of the Mariner's Chart.

II

THE CAPTAIN

IT seems strange to me, now, that I knew him so little.
My attention, my fervent admiration, were all for
Sido and only fitfully strayed from her. It was just the
same with my father. His eyes dwelt on Sido. On thinking
it over I believe that she did not know him well either.
She was content with a few broad and clumsy truths: his
love for her was boundless—it was in trying to enrich her
that he lost her fortune—she loved him with an unwaver-
ing love, treating him lightly in everyday matters but
respecting all his decisions.

All that was so glaringly obvious that it prevented us,
except at moments, from perceiving his character as a
man. When I was a child, what in fact did I know of him?
That he was wonderfully skilful at building me "cock-
chafers' houses" with glazed windows and doors, and
boats too. That he sang. That he handed out to us—and
hid too—coloured pencils, white paper, rosewood rulers,
gold dust and big, white sealing-wafers which I ate by the
fistful. That he swam with his one leg faster and better
than his rivals with all four limbs.

But I knew also that, outwardly at least, he took little
interest in his children. "Outwardly", I say. Since those
days I have pondered much on the curious shyness of
fathers in their relations with their children. Mine was
never at ease with my mother's two eldest children by her
first marriage—a girl with her head always full of
romantic visions of heroes, so lost in legends that she
was hardly present, and a boy who looked haughty but was

secretly affectionate. He was naïve enough to believe that you can conquer a child with presents. He refused to recognise in his son, the "lazzarone" as my mother called him, his own carefree musical extravagances. I was the one he set most store by, and I was still quite small when he began to appeal to my critical sense. Later on, thank goodness, I proved less precocious, but I well remember how severe a judge I was at ten years old.

"Listen to this," my father would say, and I would listen, very sternly. Perhaps it would be a purple passage of oratorical prose, or an ode in flowing verse, with a great parade of rhythm and rhyme, resounding as a mountain storm.

"Well?" my father would ask. "I really believe that this time. . . . Go on, say!"

I would toss my head with its fair plaits, a forehead too high to look amiable, and a little marble of a chin, and let fall my censure: "Too many adjectives, as usual!"

At that my father exploded, thundering abuse on me: I was dust, vermin, a conceited louse. But the vermin, unperturbed, went on: "I told you the same thing last week, about the *Ode à Paul Bert*. Too many adjectives!"

No doubt he laughed at me behind my back, and I daresay he felt proud of me too. But at the moment we glared at each other as equals, already on a fraternal footing. There can be no doubt that it is his influence I am under when music or a display of dancing—not words, never words!—move me to tears. And it was he, longing to express himself, who inspired my first fumbling attempts to write, and earned for me that most biting, and assuredly most useful praise from my husband. "Can it be that I've married the last of the lyric poets?"

Nowadays I am wise enough, and proud enough too, to distinguish what in me is my father's lyricism, and

what my mother's humour and spontaneity, all mingled
and superimposed; and to rejoice in a dichotomy in
which there is nothing and no one to blush for on either
side.

Yes, all we four children certainly made my father
uncomfortable. How can it be otherwise in families where
the father, though almost past the age for passion, remains
in love with his mate? All his life long we had disturbed
the tête-à-tête of which he had dreamed. Sometimes a
pedagogic turn of mind can draw a father closer to his
children. In the absence of affection, which is much
rarer than is generally admitted, the vainglorious pleasure
of teaching may bind a man to his sons. But Jules-Joseph
Colette, though a cultivated man, made no parade of any
learning. He had at first enjoyed shining for "Her", but
as his love increased, he came to abandon even his desire
to dazzle Sido.

I could go straight to the corner of our garden where
the snowdrops bloomed. And I could paint from
memory the climbing rose, and the trellis that supported
it, as well as the hole in the wall and the worn flagstone.
But I can only see my father's face vaguely and inter-
mittently. He is clear enough sitting in the big, rep-
covered armchair. The two oval mirrors of his open
pince-nez gleam on his chest, and the red line of his
peculiar lower lip, like a rolled rim, protrudes a little
beneath the moustache which joins his beard. In that
position he is fixed for ever.

But elsewhere he is a wandering, floating figure, full of
gaps, obscured by clouds and only visible in patches. I
can always see his white hands, particularly since I've
begun to hold my thumb bent out awkwardly, as he did,
and found my hands crumpling and rolling and destroy-
ing paper with explosive rage, just as his hands used to.

And talking of anger! But I won't enlarge on my own rages which I inherit from him. One has only to go to Saint-Sauveur, and see the state to which my father reduced the marble chimney-piece there, with two kicks from his one foot.

I disentangle those things in me that come from my father, and those that are my mother's share. Captain Colette never kissed children; his daughter maintains that a kiss destroys their bloom. But if he did not often kiss me, at least he tossed me in the air, right up to the ceiling, which I warded off with both hands and knees, shrieking with delight. He had great muscular strength, controlled and dissimulated like a cat's, and no doubt it was maintained by a frugality which disconcerted our good neighbours in Lower Burgundy: bread, coffee, lots of sugar, half-a-glass of wine, any amount of tomatoes and aubergines. When he was past seventy he consented to take a little meat, as a remedy. And sedentary though his life was, this southerner, with his satiny white skin, never put on flesh.

"Italian! Knife-man!" were the names my mother used to call him, when she was displeased with him, or when this faithful lover of hers suddenly revealed his outrageous jealousy. And it is a fact that, though he may never have killed anyone, my father always carried in his pocket a dagger whose horn handle concealed a spring. He despised firearms.

When he worked himself up into one of those sham southern rages, he would give vent to growls and high-sounding oaths to which we paid not the slightest attention. But how I trembled, on one occasion, at the melodious tone of his voice in genuine fury! I was eleven at the time.

My mysterious half-sister had recently married by her

own choice, so unwisely and unhappily that she had
nothing left to hope for but death. She swallowed some
kind of tablets and a neighbour came to tell my mother.
In twenty-odd years my father and sister had never grown
fond of each other. But at the sight of Sido suffering,
without raising his voice and in the most honeyed tones,
my father said:

"Go and tell *my* daughter's husband, tell Doctor R.,
that if he does not save that child, by evening he will have
ceased to live."

The suavity of his voice thrilled me. It was a wonderful sound, full and musical as the song of an angry sea.
If it had not been for Sido's grief, I should have run
dancing back to the garden, cheerfully hoping for the
richly-deserved death of Doctor R.

He was not only misunderstood, but unappreciated.
"That incorrigible gaiety of yours!" my mother would
exclaim, not in reproach but astonishment. She thought
he was gay because he sang. But I who whistle whenever
I am sad, and turn the pulsations of fever, or the syllables
of a name that torments me, into endless variations on a
theme, could wish she had understood that pity is the
supreme insult. My father and I have no use for pity; our
nature rejects it. And now the thought of my father
tortures me, because I know that he possessed a virtue
more precious than any facile charms: that of knowing full
well why he was sad, and never revealing it.

It is true that he often made us laugh, that he told a
good tale, embroidering recklessly when he got into the
swing of it, and that melody bubbled out of him; but did
I ever see him gay? Wherever he went, his song preceded
and protected him.

"Golden sunbeams, balmy breezes . . ." he would carol as
he walked down our deserted street, so that "She" should
not guess, when she heard him coming, that Laroche, the
Lamberts' farmer, was impudently refusing to pay his
rent, and that one of this same Lambert's creatures had
advanced my father—at seven per cent interest for six
months—a sum he could not do without.

> *By what enchantment, say, didst thou my heart beguile?*
> *When now I thee behold, methinks it was thy smile.*

Who in the world could have believed that this baritone, still nimble with the aid of crutch and stick, is
projecting his song like a smoke-screen in front of him,
so as to detract attention from himself? He sings in the
hope that perhaps to-day "She" will forget to ask him if
he has been able to borrow a hundred louis on the
security of his disabled officer's pension. When he sings,
Sido listens to him in spite of herself, and does not
interrupt him.

> *This is the trysting-place of dames and knights,*
> *Who gather here within this charming glade,*
> *To pass their days in tasting the delights* (twice)
> *Of sparkling wine and love beneath the shade!* (three times).

If, when he comes to the *grupetto*, the final long-drawn
organ note with a few high staccato notes added for fun,
he throws his voice right up against the walls of the Rue de
l'Hospice, my mother will appear on the doorstep,
scandalised but laughing:

"Oh, Colette! In the street!" and after that he has only
to fire off two or three everyday ribaldries at one of the
neighbouring young women, and Sido will pucker

those sparse Mona Lisa eyebrows of hers and banish from her mind the painful refrain that never passes her lips: "We shall have to sell the Forge ... sell the Forge ... Heavens, must we sell the Forge, as well as the Mées, the Choslins and the Lamberts?"

Gay indeed, what real reason had he to be gay? Just as in his youth he had desired to die gloriously in public, now he needed to live surrounded by warm approval. Reduced now to his village and his family, his whole being absorbed by the great love that bounded his horizon, he was most himself with strangers and distant friends. One of his old comrades-in-arms, Colonel Godchot, who is still alive, has kept Captain Colette's letters and repeats sayings of his. For this man who talked so readily was strangely silent about one thing: he never related his military exploits. It was Captain Fournès and private Lefèvre, both of the First Zouaves, who repeated to Colonel Godchot some of my father's "sayings" at the time of the war with Italy in 1859. My father, then twenty-nine years old, fell before Melegnano, his left thigh shot away. Fournès and Lefèvre dashed forward and carried him back, asking: "Where would you like us to put you, Captain?"

"In the middle of the square, under the colours!"

He never told any of his family of those words, never spoke of that hour when he hoped to die, in the midst of the tumult and surrounded by the love of his men. Nor did he ever tell any of us how he had lain alongside "his old Marshal" (Mac-Mahon). In talking to me he never referred to the one long illness I had. But now, twenty years after his death, I find that his letters are full of my name, and of the "little one's" illness.

Too late, too late! That is always the cry of children, of the negligent and the ungrateful. Not that I consider myself more guilty than any other "child", on the contrary. But while he was alive, ought I not to have seen through his humorous dignity and his feigned frivolity? Were we not worthy, he and I, of a mutual effort to know each other better?

HE was a poet and a townsman. The country, where my mother seemed to draw sustenance from the sap of all growing things, and to take on new life whenever in stooping she touched the earth, blighted my father, who behaved as though he were in exile there.

We were sometimes scandalised by the sociability which urged him into village politics and local councils, made him stand for the district council and attracted him to those assemblies and regional committees where the human voice provokes an answering human roar. Most unfairly, we felt vaguely vexed with him for not being sufficiently like the rest of us, whose joy it was to be far from the madding crowd.

I realise now that he was trying to please us when he used to organise "country picnics", as townsfolk do. The old blue victoria transported the family, with the dogs and eatables, to the banks of some pool—Moutiers, Chassaing, or the lovely little forest lake of Guillemette which belonged to us. My father was so much imbued with the "Sunday feeling", that urban need to celebrate one day out of seven, that he provided himself with fishing-rods and camp-stools.

On arrival at the pool he would adopt a jovial mood quite different from his weekday jovial mood. He uncorked the bottle of wine gaily, allowed himself an hour's fishing, read, and took a short nap, while the rest of us, light-footed woodlanders that we were, used to scouring the countryside without a carriage, were as bored as could be, sighing, as we ate cold chicken, for our accustomed snacks of new bread, garlic and cheese. The open forest, the pool and the wide sky filled my father with enthusiasm, but only as a noble spectacle. The more he called to mind *"the blue Titaresus and the silver gulf"*, the more taciturn did we become—the two boys and I, that is—, for we were already accustomed to express our worship of the woods by silence alone.

Only my mother, sitting beside the pool, between her husband and her children, seemed to derive a melancholy pleasure from counting her dear ones as they lay about her on the fine, reedy grass, purple with heather. Far from the importunate sound of doorbells, from the anxious, unpaid tradesmen, and insinuating voices, there she was with her achievement and her torment—with the exception of her faithless elder daughter—enclosed within a perfect circle of birches and oaks. Flurries of wind in the treetops passed over the circular clearing, rarely rippling the water. Domes of pinky mushrooms broke through the light silver-grey soil where the heather thrived, and my mother talked about the things that she and I loved best.

She told of the wild boars of bygone winters, of the wolves still known to exist in Puysaie and Forterre, and of the lean summer wolf which once followed the victoria for five hours. "If only I had known what to give him to eat! I daresay he would have eaten bread. Every time we came to a slope he would sit down to let the carriage keep fifty yards ahead. The scent of him made the mare mad, so much so that it was nearly she who attacked him."

"Weren't you frightened?"

"Frightened? No, not of that poor, big, grey wolf, thirsty and famished under a leaden sun. Besides, I was with my first husband. It was my first husband, too, who saw the fox drowning its fleas one day when he was out shooting. Holding on to a bunch of weeds with its teeth, it lowered itself backwards into the water very, very gradually until it was in right up to its muzzle."

Innocent tales and maternal instructions, such as the swallow, the mother-hare and the she-cat also impart to their young. Delightful stories of which my father retained only the words "my first husband", at which he would bend on Sido that grey-blue gaze of his whose meaning no one could ever fathom. In any case, what did the fox and the lily of the valley, the ripe berry and the insect, matter to him? He liked them in books, and told us their learned names, but passed them by out of doors without recognising them. He would praise any full-blown flower as a "rose", pronouncing the o short, in the Provençal way, and squeezing as he spoke an invisible "roz" between his thumb and forefinger.

Dusk descended at last on our Sunday-in-the-country. By then our number had often dropped from five to three: my father, my mother and I. The circular rampart of darkling woods had swallowed up those two lanky, bony lads, my brothers.

"We shall catch them up on the road home," my father would say.

But my mother shook her head: her boys never returned except by cross-country paths and swampy blue meadows; and then, cutting across sand-pits and bramble-patches, they would jump over the wall at the bottom of the garden. She was resigned to the prospect of finding them at home, bleeding a little and a little ragged. She gathered up from the grass the remains of the meal, a few freshly-picked mushrooms, the empty tit's nest, the springy, cellular sponge made by a colony of wasps, the bunch of wild flowers, some pebbles bearing the imprint of fossilised ammonites, and the "little one's" wide-brimmed hat, while my father, still agile, jumped with a hop like a wader's back into the victoria.

It was my mother who patted the black mare, offering

her yellowed teeth tender shoots, and wiped the paws of
the paddling dog. I never saw my father touch a horse.
No curiosity ever impelled him to look at a cat or give
his attention to a dog. And no dog ever obeyed him.

"Go on, get in!" his beautiful voice would order Mof-
fino. But the dog remained where he was by the step of the
carriage, wagging his tail coldly and looking at my mother.

"Get in, you brute! What are you waiting for?" my
father repeated. "I'm waiting for the *command*," the dog
seemed to reply.

"Go on, jump!" I would call to him; and there was
never any need to tell him twice.

"That's very odd", my mother would remark, to which
my father retorted: "It merely proves what a stupid
creature the dog is." But the rest of us did not believe a
word of that, and at heart my father felt secretly
humiliated.

Great bunches of yellow broom fanned out like a
peacock's tail behind us in the hood of the old victoria.
As we approached the village, my father would resume
his defensive humming, and no doubt we looked very
happy, since to look happy was the highest compliment
we paid each other. But was not everything about us, the
gathering dusk, the wisps of smoke trailing across the
sky, and the first flickering star, as grave and restless as
ourselves? And in our midst a man, banished from the
elements that had once sustained him, brooded bitterly.

Yes, bitterly; I am sure of that now. It takes time for the
absent to assume their true shape in our thoughts. After
death they take on a firmer outline and then cease to
change. "So that's the real you? Now I see, I'd never
understood you." It is never too late, since now I have
fathomed what formerly my youth hid from me: my
brilliant, cheerful father harboured the profound sadness

of those who have lost a limb. We were hardly aware that
one of his legs was missing, amputated just below the
hip. What should we have said if we had suddenly seen
him walking like everyone else?

Even my mother had never known him other than
supported by crutches, agile though he was and radiant
with the arrogance of one in love. But she knew nothing,
apart from his military exploits, of the man he was before
he met her, the Saint-Cyr cadet who danced so well,
the lieutenant tough as what in my native province we
call a *bois-debout*—the ancient chopping-block, made of
a roundel of close-grained oak that defies the axe. When
she followed him with her eyes she had no idea that this
cripple had once been able to run to meet every danger.
And now, bitterly, his spirit still soared, while he
remained sitting beside Sido with a sweet song on his lips.

Sido and his love for her were all that he had been able
to keep. For him, all that surrounded them—the village,
the fields and the woods—was but a desert. He supposed
that life went on for his distant friends and comrades.
Once he returned from a trip to Paris with moist eyes
because Davout d'Auerstaedt, Grand Chancellor of the
Legion of Honour, had removed his red ribbon in order
to replace it by a rosette.

"Couldn't you have asked me for it, old chap?"

"I never asked for the ribbon either", my father
answered lightly.

But his voice, when he described the scene to us, was
husky. What was the source of his emotion? He wore the
rosette, amply displayed in his button-hole, sitting up
very straight in our old carriage with his arm lying on the
cross-bar of his crutch. He would start showing off on the
outskirts of the village, for the benefit of the first passers-
by at Gerbaude. Was he dreaming of his old comrades

in the division who marched without crutches and rode by on horseback, of Février and Désandré, and Fournès who had saved his life and still tactfully addressed him as "my Captain"? Had he a vision of learned societies, of politics perhaps, and platforms, and all their dazzling symbols; a vision of masculine joys?

"You're so human!" my mother would sometimes say to him, with a note of indefinable suspicion in her voice. And so as not to wound him too much, she would add: "You know what I mean, you always put your hand out to see if it's raining."

His anecdotes were inclined to be ribald, but my mother's presence was enough to check the Toulon or Africa story on his lips. And although her own speech was piquant, she modestly toned it down in front of him. But sometimes when she was not thinking, she got carried away by a familiar rhythm and surprised herself quietly singing bugle calls whose words had been handed down unaltered from the imperial to the republican armies.

"Now we needn't feel embarrassed any longer," remarked my father from behind the outspread sheets of *Le Temps*.

"Oh," gasped my mother, "I only hope the child didn't hear."

"Oh, the child, it doesn't matter about her," retorted my father. And he would fasten on his chosen one that extraordinary, challenging, grey-blue gaze of his, which revealed his secrets to no one, though sometimes admitting that such secrets existed.

When I am alone I try to imitate that look of my father's. Sometimes I succeed fairly well, especially when

I use it to face up to some hidden hurt, which proves
how efficacious insult can be against something that has
you in its power, and how great is the pleasure of standing
up to a tyrant: "You may cause my death in the end, but
I shall take as long as possible over it, never fear."

"Oh, the child, it doesn't matter about her." Well, that
was frank enough, and what a challenge to his one and
only love! All the same he liked me for certain characteristics in which, had he seen me more clearly, he might
have recognised himself. Little by little he was losing the
gift of observation and the power of comparison. I was
not more than thirteen when I noticed that my father was
ceasing to see, in the physical sense of the word, his
Sido herself.

"Another new dress?" he would exclaim with surprise.
"Bless my soul, Madam!"

Taken aback, Sido would round on him in earnest:
"New? Oh come now, Colette, where are your eyes?"
With two fingers she would take hold of the worn silk
of a "Sunday best" embroidered with jet. "I've had it
three years, Colette! D'you hear what I say? It's three
years old! And there's life in it yet!" she added quickly,
with a note of pride in her voice. "Dyed navy blue . . ."

But he was no longer listening to her. He had already
jealously rejoined her in some favourite spot, where she
wore a chignon with Victorian side-curls, and a bodice
with tulle ruching and a heart-shaped opening at the
neck. As he grew older he could not even bear her to look
tired or to be ill. "Keep on now, keep on!" he would urge
her, as though she were a horse that only he had the right
to overwork. And she kept on.

I never surprised them in a passionate embrace.
Who had imposed such reserve on them? Sido, most

assuredly. My father would have had no such scruples about it. Always on the alert where she was concerned, he used to listen for her quick step, and bar her way:

"Pay up, or I won't let you pass!" he would order, pointing to the smooth patch of cheek above his beard. Pausing in her flight, she would "pay" with a kiss as swift as a sting, and speed on her way, irritated if my brothers or I had seen her "paying".

Only once, on a summer day, when my mother was removing the coffee-tray from the table, did I see my father, instead of exacting the familiar toll, bend his greying head and bearded lips over my mother's hand with a devotion so ardent and ageless that Sido, speechless and as crimson with confusion as I, turned away without a word. I was still a child and none too pure-minded, being exercised as one is at thirteen by all those matters concerning which ignorance is a burden and discovery humiliating. It did me good to behold, and every now and again to remember afresh, that perfect picture of love: the head of a man already old, bent in a kiss of complete self-surrender on a graceful, wrinkled little hand, worn with work.

For a long time he was terrified lest she should die before he did. This is a thought common to lovers and truly-devoted married people, a cruel hope that excludes any idea of pity. Before my father's death, Sido used to talk of him to me:

"I mustn't die before him, I simply must not. Can't you imagine how, if I let myself die, he'd try to kill himself, and fail? I know him," she said, with the air of a young girl. She mused for a while, her eyes on the little street of Châtillon-Coligny, or the enclosed square of our garden. "There's less chance of that with me, you see. I'm only a woman and, once past a certain age, a woman practically never dies of her own free will. Besides, I've got you as well and he hasn't."

For she knew everything, even to those preferences that one never mentions. Far from being any support to us, my father was merely one of the cluster that clung round her and hung on to her arms.

She fell ill and he sat often near the bed. "When are you going to get well? What day, what time do you think it will be? Don't you dare not to recover! I should soon put an end to my life!" She could not bear this masculine attitude, so threatening and pitiless in its demands. In her effort to escape, she turned her head from side to side on her pillow, as she was to do later when she was shaking off the last ties.

"My goodness, Colette, you're making me so hot!" she complained. "You fill the whole room. A man's always out of place at a woman's bedside. Go out of doors! Go and see if the grocer's got any oranges for me. Go and ask Monsieur Rosimond to lend me the *Revue des Deux-Mondes*. But go slowly, because it's thundery, otherwise you'll come back in a sweat!"

Thrusting his crutch up under his armpit, he did as she bade.

"D'you see?" said my mother, when he had gone, "d'you notice how all the stuffing goes out of him when I'm ill?"

As he passed beneath her window he would clear his throat so that she could hear him:

> "*I think of thee, I see thee, I adore thee,*
> *At every moment, always, everywhere,*
> *My thoughts are of thee when the sun is rising,*
> *And when I close my eyes thy face is there.*"

"D'you hear him? D'you hear him?" she would say feverishly. Then her sense of mischief got the upper hand, making her whole face suddenly younger, and leaning out of bed she would say: "Would you like to know what your father is? I'll tell you. Your father is the modern Orpheus!"

She recovered, as she always did. But when they removed one of her breasts and, four years later, the other, my father became terribly mistrustful of her, even though each time she recovered again. When a fish-bone stuck in her throat, making her cough so violently that her face turned scarlet and her eyes filled with tears, my father brought his fist down on the table, shivering his plate to fragments and bellowing: "Stop it, I say!"

She was not misled by this, and she soothed him with compassionate tact, and comic remarks, and fluttering glances. The words "fluttering glance" always come to my lips when I am thinking of her. Hesitation, the desire to say something tender, and the need to tell a lie, all made her flutter her eyelids while her grey eyes glanced rapidly in all directions. This confusion, and the vain attempt of those eyes to escape from a man's gaze, blue-grey as new-cut lead, was all that was revealed to me of the passion which bound Sido and the Captain throughout their lives.

ONE day, ten years ago, at the suggestion of a friend I called at the house of Madame B., whose professional business is with "spirits". That is her word for what remains, in the air about us, of the departed, particularly of those who were closely bound to us by ties of blood and love. It must not be thought that I cherish any particular belief, nor even that I take special pleasure in the company of those privileged persons who are gifted with second sight. It is merely my curiosity, always the same, which impels me to go and see, indiscriminately and one after the other, Madame B., the "woman-with-the-candle," the dog-who-can-count, the rose-bush with edible fruit, the doctor who adds human blood to my human blood, and I don't know what else. If ever I lose that curiosity you may as well bury me, for I shall have ceased to exist. One of my latest imprudences was concerned with the big hymenoptera of blue steel which abounds in Provence from July to August, when the sunflowers are in bloom. Vexed at not knowing the name of this steel-clad warrior, I kept asking myself: "Has he or has he not got a sting? Is he merely a magnificent but sabreless samurai?" It is a great relief to have this uncertainty removed. A funny little disfigurement on the middle joint of one of my fingers is proof that the blue warrior is not only superbly armed, but quick on the draw.

At Madame B.'s I was agreeably surprised to find a modern, sunlit apartment. Birds were singing in a cage in the window, and children laughing in the next room. A pleasant, plump woman with white hair assured me that she had no need either of dim lights or a sinister setting. All she wanted was a moment of meditation, with my hand held between both of hers.

"Are there any questions you would like to put to me?" she asked. I realised then that I was quite without any eagerness or desire for another world of any kind, or indeed any excessive wishes, and the only question I could think of was the commonplace: "So you see the dead, do you? What do they look like?"

"Like the living," Madame B. answered briskly. "Behind you, for instance . . ."

Behind me was the sunlit window and the cage of green canaries.

". . . behind you the 'spirit' of an old man is sitting. He has a spreading, untrimmed beard, nearly white, and rather long, grey hair, brushed back. His eyebrows—my word, what eyebrows, extraordinarily bushy—and as for the eyes under them! They're small, but so brilliant one can hardly endure their gaze. Have you any idea who it might be?"

"Yes, indeed I have."

"In any case he's a spirit in very good circumstances."

"?"

"In very good circumstances in the spirit world. He's very much taken up with you. . . . Don't you believe it?"

"I rather doubt it."

"Well he is. He's very much taken up with you *at present.*"

"Why at present?"

"Because you represent what he would so much have liked to be when he was on earth. You are exactly what he longed to be. But he himself was never able."

I shall not mention here the other portraits which Madame B. painted for me. Everyone of them was remarkable, in my eyes, for some detail so striking and private that I was enchanted as though by a harmless and

inexplicable piece of sorcery. Of one "spirit" in whom I
could not but recognise, feature by feature, my elder half-
brother, she said compassionately: "I've never seen a
dead person so sad!"

"But", I asked her, vaguely jealous, "don't you see an
old woman who might be my mother?"

Madame B.'s kind glance wandered all round me. "No,
I can't say I do", she finally answered, adding quickly, as
if to comfort me, "Perhaps she's resting. That does
happen sometimes. Are you the only child left? (*sic*)"

"I still have one brother."

"That's it!" exclaimed Madame B., kindly. "No doubt
she's busy with him. A spirit can't be everywhere at once
you know."

I did not know. During the same visit I learned that
intercourse with the departed is not hampered by daylight or everyday fun. "They're like the living," asserts
Madame B., serene in her faith. Why not? Like the living
except that they are dead. Dead—that's all. That was why
she was astonished to see in my elder brother a dead
person "so sad". But doubtless she was seeing him,
through the transparent veil of my subconscious, as I
had seen him when he was as though battered with blows
by his last painful journey, careworn still and utterly
exhausted, most sad indeed.

As for my father . . . "You are exactly what he longed
to be, and in his lifetime he was never able." There
indeed is something for me to brood upon, something
to touch my heart. I can still see, on one of the highest
shelves of the library, a row of volumes bound in boards,
with black linen spines. The firmness of the boards, so
smoothly covered in marbled paper, bore witness to
my father's manual dexterity. But the titles, handwritten
in Gothic lettering, never tempted me, more especially

since the black-rimmed labels bore no author's name. I
quote from memory: *My Campaigns, The Lessons of '70,
The Geodesy of Geodesies, Elegant Algebra, Marshal Mac-
Mahon seen by a Fellow-Soldier, From Village to Parliament,
Zouave Songs* (in verse) . . . I forget the rest.

When my father died, the library became a bedroom
and the books left their shelves.

"Just come and see," my elder brother called one day.
In his silent way, he was moving the books himself,
sorting and opening them in search of a smell of damp-
stained paper, of that embalmed mildew from which a
vanished childhood rises up, or the pressed petal of a tulip
still marbled like a tree-agate.

"Just come and see!"

The dozen volumes bound in boards revealed to us
their secret, a secret so long disdained by us, accessible
though it was. Two hundred, three hundred, one
hundred and fifty pages to a volume; beautiful, cream-
laid paper, or thick "foolscap" carefully trimmed,
hundreds and hundreds of blank pages. Imaginary works,
the mirage of a writer's career.

There were so many of these virgin pages, spared
through timidity or listlessness, that we never saw the end
of them. My brother wrote his prescriptions on them, my
mother covered her pots of jam with them, her grand-
daughters tore out the leaves for scribbling, but we never
exhausted those cream-laid notebooks, his invisible
"works". All the same my mother exerted herself to
that end with a sort of fever of destruction: "You don't
mean to say there are still some left? I must have some
for cutlet-frills. I must have some to line my little drawers
with . . ." And this not in mockery but out of piercing
regret and the painful desire to blot out this proof of
incapacity.

At the time when I was beginning to write, I too drew on this spiritual legacy. Was that where I got my extravagant taste for writing on smooth sheets of fine paper, without the least regard for economy? I dared to cover with my large round handwriting the invisible cursive script, perceptible to only one person in the world like a shining tracery which carried to a triumphant conclusion the single page lovingly completed and signed, the page that bore the dedication:

TO MY DEAR SOUL,

HER FAITHFUL HUSBAND:

JULES-JOSEPH COLETTE.

III

THE SAVAGES

"SAVAGES, that's what they are," my mother used to say, "just savages. What can one do with such savages?" And she would shake her head.

Her discouragement was in part due to a deliberate and considered refusal to interfere, and in part perhaps to an awareness of her own responsibility. She gazed at her two boys, the half-brothers, and found them beautiful, especially the elder, the seventeen-year-old with his chestnut hair and clear blue eyes, and that crimson mouth which smiled only at us and a few pretty girls. But the dark one, at thirteen, was not bad either, with his hair that needed a cut falling into his lead-blue eyes, that were like our father's.

Two light-footed savages, lean and bony, frugal like their parents; instead of meat preferring brown bread, hard cheese, salads, fresh eggs, and leek or pumpkin pies. Temperate and pure they were—true savages indeed.

"What shall I do with them?" sighed my mother. By their very gentleness they evaded all attempts to interfere with them, or separate them. The elder was the leader, while the younger mingled with his enthusiasm a sense of fantasy which cut him off from the world. But the elder knew he was soon to begin his medical studies, whereas the younger dumbly hoped that for him nothing ever would begin, except the next day, except the hour when he could escape from civilised constraint, except complete freedom to dream and remain silent. He is hoping still.

They rarely played, unless indeed it was a kind of game

to spurn all but the flower, the cream of that radiant village-world, and choose only the most solitary, the untrodden ways, all that renews its youth and springs afresh far from the haunts of men. One never saw them dressed up like Robinson Crusoe, or disguised as warriors, or acting plays they had made up themselves. On one occasion when the younger joined a group of stage-struck boys, the only part he would accept was a silent one: the part of the "idiot boy".

I have to go back to my mother's stories when, like all of us as we grow older, I am seized with the itch to possess the secrets of a being who has vanished for ever: to discover the "key" to his turbulent youth, each hour of it swallowed up by the succeeding hour, yet perpetually renewing itself; to point, thanks to some miraculous guidance, with absolute certainty to that high place whence he allowed himself to fall down to the dead level of mankind; and to spell out the names of his evil stars.

I have said farewell to the dead, to the peerless elder brother; but I turn to my mother's stories, and to the memories of my own earliest childhood, when I want to find out what went to the making of the sixty-year-old with the grey moustache who glides into my home at nightfall, opens my watch to see the second-hand flipping round, cuts a foreign stamp from a crumpled envelope, inhales, as though he had been short of breath all day, a long draught of music from the gramophone, and disappears without having said a word.

That greying man has grown out of a little boy of six, who used to follow mendicant musicians when they passed through our village. Once he followed a one-eyed clarinettist as far as Saints, a distance of four miles, and by the time he got back my mother was having all the local wells dragged. He listened good-naturedly to her

reproaches and complaints, for he rarely lost his temper.
When he had heard the last of his mother's fears, he went
to the piano and faithfully reproduced all the clarinettist's
tunes, enriching them with simple but perfectly correct
little harmonies. He did the same with the tunes of
the roundabout at the Easter fair on Low Sunday, and
indeed with any kind of music, which he would intercept as though it were a flying message.

"He must study technique and harmony," my mother
would say. "He's even more gifted than his elder brother.
He might become an artiste; who can tell?"

When he was six she still believed that she had it in her
power to help or hinder him. He was such an inoffensive
little boy, she could find no fault with him, except his
tendency to disappear. Small of stature, agile, and very
well balanced, by some magic he was suddenly not
present. Where to find him? The favourite haunts of
the ordinary small boys—the skating-rink and the Place
du Grand-Jeu pounded flat by childish feet—had not
even seen him pass their way. He was more likely to be
found in the ancient cold-storage room of the castle, a
rough-hewn vault four centuries old, or in the case of
the town clock in the Place du Marché, or else dogging
the piano-tuner who came once a year from the county
town to attend to the four "instruments" in our village.
"What make is your instrument?" "Madame Vallée's
going to exchange her instrument", "Mademoiselle
Philippon's instrument is worn out!"

Even now, I confess, the word "instrument" still
conjures up in my memory, to the exclusion of all other
images, that of a mahogany construction preserved in
dim provincial parlours, and brandishing, like an altar,
two bronze arms with green candles.

Yes indeed, an inoffensive little boy who never made

any demands, except one evening when he said: "I'd
like a pennyworth of dried plums and a pennyworth of
hazel-nuts."

"The grocers are closed," my mother answered. "Go
to sleep now and you shall have some to-morrow."

The next evening the gentle little boy asked again:
"I'd like a pennyworth of dried plums and a pennyworth
of hazel-nuts."

"Why ever didn't you buy them during the day?"
my mother exclaimed impatiently. "Go to bed!"

The next five or ten evenings brought the same teasing,
and my mother amply proved what an exceptional
mother she was. For she did not spank the persistent
child, who was perhaps hoping that she would, or at
least counting on a maternal outburst of cries, due to
exasperated nerves, and maledictions—an evening uproar
which would postpone bedtime. One evening after many
such, he assumed the routine expression of childish
obstinacy and his reasonable tone of voice: "Mother?"

"Yes", mother answered.

"Mother, I'd like . . ."

"Here they are," said she. She got up, fetched for him,
from the bottomless cupboard next to the chimney-piece,
two sacks as big as new-born babes, set them down on
each side of her little boy and remarked: "When those are
finished, you can buy some more."

He looked up at her, pale and offended beneath his
black hair. "It's for you, take it," my mother insisted.
He was the first to lose his composure, and he burst
into tears: "But . . . but . . . I don't like them!" he
sobbed.

Sido bent over him, as attentive as if he were an egg
cracking as it began to hatch, or an unknown variety of
rose, or a messenger from the other hemisphere:

"You don't like them? Then what was it you wanted?"
Rashly he confessed: "I wanted to ask for them."

Every three months my mother used to go to Auxerre,
and when she was setting out in the victoria at two in the
morning, she nearly always gave in to the pleadings of
the baby of the family. The good fortune of being born
last allowed me to keep for a long time this privileged
position of being the baby-of-the-family, and my place
in the back seat of the victoria. But before me it had been
occupied for ten years by that agile and elusive little boy.
On arrival at the county town he always vanished,
evading every attempt to keep an eye on him. He disappeared all over the place, in the cathedral, in the clock
tower, and especially in a big grocer's shop while they
were packing up the sugar-loaf in its oblique wrapping of
indigo paper, the ten pounds of chocolate, the vanilla,
the cinnamon, the nutmeg, the rum for grog, the black
pepper and the white soap. My mother gave the shrill
cry of a vixen: "Hi! Where is he?"
"Who, Madame Colette?"
"My little boy! Did anyone see him go out?"
No one had seen him go out, and since there were no
wells, my mother was already peering into the vats of
oil and the casks of pickled brine.
This time it did not take them long to find him. He was
up near the ceiling, right at the top of one of the cast-iron
spiral pillars. Gripping this between his thighs and feet,
like a native up a coconut-palm, he was fiddling with
and listening to the works of a big, hanging clock with a
flat, owl face, which was screwed on to the main beam.
When ordinary parents produce exceptional children,

they are often so dazzled by them that they push them into careers that they consider superior, even if it takes some lusty kicks on their behinds to achieve this result. My mother found it quite natural, and indeed obligatory, that the children she had produced should be miracles; but it was also her view that "God helps those who help themselves", and to reassure herself she was given to asserting: "Achille will be a doctor. But Léo will never get away from music. As for the little one . . ." At that point she would raise her eyebrows, interrogate the clouds, and postpone me till later.

The strange exception was my elder sister, about whose future there was never any discussion, although she was already of age. But she was a stranger to us, and indeed to everyone, isolated by her own choice in the bosom of her own family.

"Juliette is a different kind of savage," my mother sighed. "A kind that no one can understand, not even I."

She was wrong about us, or rather we disappointed her, more than once. But she never lost heart; she merely supplied us with a fresh halo. All the same she could never admit that her second son had got away, as she put it, from music, for in many a letter dating from the end of her life I read: "*Do you know if Léo has any time to practise his piano? He ought not to neglect such an extraordinary gift; I shall never tire of insisting on that.*" At the time when my mother was writing me these letters, my brother was forty-four years old.

Whatever she might say, he did get away from music, then from his pharmaceutical studies, and then successively from everything—from everything except his own elfin past. To my eyes he has not changed; he is an elf of sixty-three. He is attached to nothing but his native place, like an elf to some tutelary mushroom, or a leaf bent like a roof. Elves, we know, live on very little, and despise the coarse garments of mortals: mine sometimes wanders about without a tie and with flowing locks. From behind he looks not unlike an empty overcoat, straying bewitched.

He has deliberately chosen his humble, clerical job because it keeps sitting at a table that part of himself that looks deceptively like a man. All the rest of him is free to sing, listen to orchestras, compose, and fly back to the past, to rejoin the small boy of six who opened every watch, haunted town clocks, collected epitaphs, never tired of stamping on spongy mosses, and played the piano from birth. He finds him again without difficulty, slips into the light and nimble little body that he never leaves long, and roams through a country of the mind, where all is to the measure and liking of one who for sixty years has triumphantly remained a child.

Alas, no child is invulnerable, and this one sometimes comes back to me badly hurt because he has tried to confront his well-remembered dream with a reality which betrays it.

One dripping evening, when every arcade of the Palais-Royal was hung with great draperies of water and shadow, he came to call on me. I had not seen him for months. He sat down, wet through, beside my fire, absent-mindedly took some of his curious nourishment—fondants, very sugary cakes, and syrup—opened my watch, then my alarm-clock, listened to them for a long time and said nothing.

I stole an occasional glance at his long face with its nearly white moustache, my father's blue eyes, and a coarser version of Sido's nose—inherited features connected by bony modelling and unfamiliar muscles whose origin I could not trace. A long and gentle face it was, in the firelight, gentle and distressed. But the habits and customs of childhood—reserve, discretion and liberty—persist so strongly between us, that I asked my brother no questions.

When he had finished drying the sad, rain-sodden wings that he calls his coat, he smoked with half-shut eyes, rubbed his hands that were shrivelled and red for lack of gloves and hot water in all weathers, and spoke:

"I say!"

"Yes?"

"I've been *back there*, did you know?"

"No! When?"

"I've just returned."

"Oh!" said I with admiration. "You've been to Saint-Sauveur? How?"

He gave me a conceited little look. "Charles Faroux took me in his motor."

"My dear! Was it looking lovely at this time of year?"

"Not bad," he said, shortly.

His nostrils dilated and he relapsed into silence and gloom. I went back to my writing.

"I say!"

"Yes?"

"*Back there*, I went to Roches, you remember?"

A steep path of yellow sand rose in my memory like a serpent against a window pane. "Oh, how is it looking? And the wood at the summit? And the little pavilion? And the foxgloves . . . the heather . . ."

My brother whistled. "Gone. Cut down. Nothing left. A clean sweep. You can see the earth. You can see . . ." He scythed the air with the side of his hand and shrugged derisively, staring into the fire. I respected this derision and did not imitate it. But the old elf, quivering in his pain, could no longer keep silence. Profiting by the half-light of the glowing fire, he whispered:

"And that's not all. I went to the Cour du Pâté too."

Back to my mind you rush, childish name for a warm terrace beside a ruined castle, arches of climbing roses spindly with age, shadow and scent of flowering ivy falling from the Saracen tower, and stubborn, rusty gates that close the Cour du Pâté . . .

"And then, my dear, and then?"

My brother gathered himself together.

"Just a moment," he ordered me. "We must begin at the beginning. I arrive at the castle. It's still a home for old people, since that was what Victor Gandrille decided. That's all right, I've nothing against that. I enter the park by the lower entrance, the one near Madame Billette's . . ."

"Surely not Madame Billette? Why, she must have been dead for at least fifty years!"

"Maybe," said my brother with indifference. "Yes, I suppose that's why they told me another name . . . an impossible name. If *they* think I'm going to remember names I don't know! Well then, I enter by the lower entrance and go up the lime avenue. Now I come to think of it, the dogs didn't bark when I pushed the door open . . ." he remarked irritably.

"Come now, my dear, they couldn't have been the same dogs. Just think."

"All right, all right . . . it's a mere detail. I'll say nothing about the potatoes that *they*'ve planted in place of the bleeding hearts and poppies. I won't even mention," he went on in an intolerant voice, "the wiring round the lawns, a fence of wire-netting . . . you can hardly believe your eyes. It appears it's for the cows. The cows!"

He rocked one of his knees between his clasped hands

and whistled with a professional air that suited him about as well as a top hat.

"And was that all, my dear?"

"Just a moment!" he said again, fiercely. "As I said, I go up towards the canal,—if indeed," he added, with studied precision, "I dare call canal that filthy pond, that soup of mosquitoes and cow-dung. But never mind. So on I go to the Cour du Pâté, and . . ."

"And?"

He turned towards me, without seeing me, with a vindictive smile.

"I'll admit that at first I wasn't particularly pleased that *they* should have turned the first court—the one before the gate and behind the stables—into a kind of drying-ground for the washing. Yes, I'll admit that! But I didn't pay much attention to it because I was waiting for 'the moment of the gate'."

"What moment of the gate?"

He snapped his fingers impatiently.

"Oh come now! You see the knob of the gate?"

I could indeed see it—of shiny, black, cast iron—as though I were about to grasp it.

"Well, as long as I've known it, when you turn it like that"—he mimicked the gesture—"and let go of the gate, it opens through its own weight and as it swings it says . . ."

"Ee-ee-ee-ang," we sang in unison, on four notes.

"That's right," said my brother, frantically jigging his left knee. "I turned it. I let the gate go. I listened. D'you know what *they*'ve done?"

"No."

"*They*'ve oiled the gate," he said coldly.

He left almost immediately. He had nothing else to say to me. He folded the damp membranes of his voluminous garment about him and took himself off, the poorer by four notes. Henceforth his musician's ear would strain in vain to catch that most delicate of offertories, composed by an ancient gate, a grain of sand, and a trace of rust, and dedicated to the one untamed child who was worthy of it.

"**W**HAT's your score with Mérimée?"
"He owes me sixpence."
"Golly!" exclaimed the elder.
"Yes, but," went on the younger, "I owe three bob back."
"What on?"
"On a Victor Hugo."
"Which one?"
"*Chansons des rues et des bois* and I forget what else. The dirty dog!"
"And what's more I'll bet you skipped," crowed the elder. "Fork out the three bob!"
"Where d'you suppose I'm going to get hold of them? I haven't a bean."
"Ask mother."
"Oh!"
"Then ask father. Tell him it's to buy cigarettes and that you're asking him unbeknownst to mother, and he'll give them to you."
"But what if he doesn't?"
"Then you'll be fined. Threepence for the delay!"
The two savages, who read as adolescents did read in those days, that is to say to excess and with frenzy, day and night, in the tops of trees and in haylofts, had put a taboo on the word *mignonne*, which they pronounced "minionne" with a hideous, twisted grimace, followed by a pretence of retching. Every *mignonne*, doomed to execration, discovered in each new book, brought a penny into the kitty. On the other hand, an "uncontaminated" book won back sixpence for its reader. The agreement had been in force for two months, and if any money remained at the end of term it would pay for beanos, butterfly-nets or a gudgeon-trap.

My youth—I was eight—excluded me from the partnership. According to my two brothers, it was too short a time since I had left off scraping the long, tear-shaped drips from the candles, so as to eat them, and the two boys still called me "the Cossack's child". All the same, I knew how to say "minionne" with a twist of my mouth, and make vomiting noises after, and I was learning how to assess novelists according to the new rulings.

"Dickens pays very good dividends," said one savage.

"Dickens oughtn't to count," the other objected. "It's a translation, and the translator defrauds us."

"Then Edgar Allen Poe doesn't count either?"

"M'm. If we were sensible we'd exclude history books too. They pay sixpence each for a dead cert. They can't say the Revolution was 'mignonne'—euhl Charlotte Corday isn't 'mignonne'—euhl Mérimée ought to be excluded because he wrote the *Chronique de Charles IX*."

"Well then, what would you do about *Le Collier de la Reine*?"

"That counts. It's a novel pure and simple."

"And the Balzacs about Catherine de Medici?"

"Don't be silly. Of course they count."

"Oh no they don't, old man, excuse me!"

"My dear old chap, on your honour now . . . Shut up, there's someone coming."

They never quarrelled. Stretched full length along the top of the wall, they would roast in the afternoon sun, arguing hotly but never slanging each other. They would allow me a place on the gently-inclined stone coping of the wall. From there we commanded the Rue des Vignes, a deserted lane leading to the kitchen gardens scattered about the valley of Saint-Jean. At the sound of footsteps, no matter how far off, my brothers would fall silent, craftily flatten themselves close against the wall, and

thrust out their chins over the primordial foe—their
fellow creature.

"It's nothing; only Chebrier going to his kitchen-
garden," announced the younger.

Forgetting their argument for a moment, they basked
in the still-warm air and the slanting light. Other footsteps, quick and distinct, rang out on the flint cobbles.
A lilac bodice and a mop of frizzy, copper-red hair lit
up the top of the street.

"Yah! the redhead!" whispered the younger. "Yah!
carrots!"

He was only fourteen and he had a grudge against "girls"
whom he found altogether too garish and dazzling.

"It's Flore Chebrier going to meet her father," said my
elder brother when the gold and lilac had faded out at the
bottom of the street. "I say, she's come on a lot!"

His junior, lying on his stomach, laid his chin on his
folded arms. He blinked disdainfully, and pouted his lips,
already as round and full as those of the little Winds on
old nautical maps.

"Carrots, that's what she is! And ginger! Fire! Fire!"
he cried rudely, like any jealous schoolboy.

The elder shrugged his shoulders. "You're no judge
of blondes," he said. "Personally, I think she's very—yes,
really very, very mignonne. . . ."

A shout of boyish laughter, in a cracked voice beginning to break, greeted the accursed word, uttered so caress-
ingly in the dreamy voice of the elder, the charmer with
the grey eyes. I heard a scuffle on the wall, the nails of
shoes scraping the stone, the soft thud of entwined bodies
falling on the yielding, freshly-hoed earth at the foot of
the apricot-trees. But good sense prevailed at once and
they let go of each other.

They never had fought or called each other names, and

I think they already knew that that mass of red hair and the lilac bodice, wonders to be had for the asking, would never be a prize worth a joint wager, or find a place among their curious and modest delights. So back they went, their steps well matched, to their cork "display boards" where the swallow-tail butterflies were drying, to the fountain they were building, and to a "system" for distilling marsh mint, an unreliable contraption which removed the scent of the mint from the distilled product, but preserved intact the smell of the marsh.

Those wild spirits of theirs were not always harmless. The age we call awkward, and the growing pains it inflicts on young bodies, exact occasional sacrifices. My brothers had to have a victim. They chose a school-fellow who used to come to the neighbouring district for the holidays. Mathieu M. had no failings and no great merits either. Friendly, nicely-dressed, rather tow-headed, the mere sight of him roused in my two brothers a wilfulness like that of a pregnant woman. And because of that he attached himself passionately to the two arrogant savages who, with their canvas shoes and their rush hats, despised his ties. The elder could find nothing harsh enough for this "scrivener's son", and the younger, following his lead and anxious to go one better, would tear holes in his handkerchief and turn his already too-short trousers up higher still, to welcome Mathieu when, neatly gloved, he descended from his tricycle.

"I've brought the score of *Les Noces de Jeannette*," the affectionate victim would call out when he was still some way off, "and the German edition of Beethoven's Symphonies, arranged as duets!"

Gloomily, the elder, the fresh-faced barbarian, would

eye the intruder, commonplace child of commonplace parents, whom no dark mood ever touched, who never harboured a longing for solitude and was a stranger to intolerance, and who now became flustered under that look and began to plead:

"Wouldn't you like to play duets for a bit with me?"

"With you, no; without you, yes."

"Then I'll turn the pages."

The one submissive and the other inexplicably spiteful and threatening, they were hopelessly incompatible; but Mathieu M., patient as an ill-used wife, never tired of coming back again.

One day the savages took themselves off immediately after lunch and did not return until evening. They seemed tired and excited, and flung themselves down, steaming hot, on the two old sofas covered in green rep.

"Where have you been to get in that state?" my mother asked.

"Miles away," the elder replied pleasantly.

"Mathieu's been here and he seemed surprised not to find you."

"It doesn't take much to surprise that chap."

When they were alone with me, my two brothers began to talk. I never counted, and besides they had brought me up never to tell tales. I learnt that, hidden in a wood overlooking the road from Saint-F., they had not revealed their presence when Mathieu went by. I was not much interested in the details they kept going over and over:

"When I heard his tricycle bell . . ." began the younger.

"Go on, I heard it much further off than you did."

"You can't prove that! D'you remember the moment when he stopped right under our noses to mop off the sweat?"

They were conversing almost in an undertone, lying on their backs with their eyes on the ceiling. The elder became excited:

"*Rather*. The beastly creature kept looking left and right as though he could smell us."

"I say, old chap, that's pretty good, isn't it? Pretty odd, I mean. D'you really think it was we who stopped him by looking at him? He certainly looked very bothered and queer."

The eyes of the elder darkened. "May be we did. He had his tartan tie on. I always thought that tie would cause an accident one day."

I flung myself between them, eager for sensation: "Go on, what happened? What accident was there?"

They both gave me the coldest of stares. "Where on earth has this creature sprung from? What's she want with her accident?"

"But it was you who just said . . ."

They got up and sat down, sniggering in collusion: "Nothing happened," said the elder at last. "What did you expect to happen? We let Mathieu go by and we had a lot of fun."

"Is that all?" I said, disappointed.

The younger leapt to his feet and began to jig up and down, no longer able to contain himself.

"Yes, that's all! You can't understand! We were lying there and we had him on a level with our chins! Him and his tie and his side-parting, his cuffs and his shiny nose! Oh my, it was spiffing!"

He bent over his elder and brushed him with his nose like a little animal: "It would have been easy to kill him, wouldn't it?"

His body tense and his eyes closed, the elder made no reply.

"And you didn't kill him?" I asked in astonishment.

No doubt it was my surprise which pulled them out of the dark wood where, unseen, they had lain in wait, trembling with homicidal pleasure, for they burst out laughing and became puerile once more, at my expense.

"No," said the elder, "we didn't kill him. But I really don't know why."

In high spirits again, he broke into his favourite improvisations, an uncouth medley of words and rhythms, the product of those hours when his student's mind, casting work aside, unconsciously sought relief in divorcing words from their meaning. My small voice echoed his, and I am the only one left now to declare, to the tune of a polka, that:

> *A cachet*
> *Of benzo-naphtol*
> *Is just the thing*
> *For a bad headache.*

> *A cachet*
> *Of benzo-naphtol*
> *Is just the thing*
> *For an inflamed neck!*

A rash assertion, contrary to all the laws of medicine, I preferred the text, if not the tune, of a familiar serenade:

> *The analgesic balm*
> *Of the pharmacist Bengué*
>   *Bengué,*
> *Is very distingué,*
> *It can't do any harm,*
> *Though it makes you feel more gay,*
>   *More gay,* etc.

That evening, my brother, still over-excited, sang the new version of the *Serenade* by Severo Torelli—

> *We didn't kill Mathieu to-night, my dear,*
> *We thought it was much too soon,*
> *So we're letting him live a bit longer,*
> *Though he's mad as the man in the moon.*

The younger boy danced round him, radiant as Lorenzaccio after his first crime. He broke off to promise me, kindly: "We'll kill him next time."

My half-sister, the eldest of us all—the stranger in our midst—got engaged just when she seemed about to become an old maid. Plain though she was, with her Tibetan eyes she was not unpleasing. My mother did not dare to prevent this unfortunate marriage, but at least she made no secret of what she thought about it. From the Rue de la Roche to Gerbaude, and from Bel-Air to Le Grand-Jeu, the talk was all of my sister's marriage.

"Is Juliette getting married?" a neighbour would ask my mother. "There's an event!"

"No, an accident," corrected Sido.

A few ventured, acidly: "So Juliette's getting married at last! How unexpected! It almost seemed hopeless!"

"I should rather say desperate," retorted Sido, belligerently. "But there's no holding a girl of twenty-five."

"And who is she marrying?"

"Oh, some wretched upstart or other."

At heart she was full of pity for her lonely daughter, who spent her days in a fever of reading, her head stuffed with dreams. My brothers considered the "event"

entirely from their own detached point of view. A year of
medical studies in Paris had by no means tamed the elder;
magnificent and aloof, he resented the glances of such
women as he did not desire. The words "bridal train",
"dress clothes", "wedding breakfast", "procession" fell
on the two savages like drops of boiling pitch.

"I won't go to the wedding!" protested the younger,
his eyes pale with indignation under his hair cropped
close as a convict's, as usual. "I won't offer anyone my
arm! I won't wear tails!"

"But you're your sister's groom of honour," my
mother pointed out to him.

"Well then, all she's got to do is not to marry! And
for what she's marrying! A chap who stinks of vermouth!
Besides, she's always got along without us, so I can't see
why she needs us to help her get married!"

Our handsome elder brother was less vocal, but we
recognised that look on his face that he always wore
when he was planning to leap over a wall, and measuring
the obstacles. There were difficult days and recriminations
which my father, full of anxiety himself and eager to avoid
the malodorous intruder, was unable to quell. Then all at
once the two boys appeared to agree to everything.
Better still, they suggested that they themselves should
organise a choral mass, and Sido was so delighted that
for a few hours she forgot her "upstart" of a son-in-
law.

Our Aucher piano was carted along to the church and
mingled its sweet but slightly tinny tone with the bleating
of the harmonium. Bolting themselves into the empty
church, the savages rehearsed the "Suite" from *l'Arlés-
ienne*, something of Stradella's and a piece by Saint-
Saens specially arranged for the nuptial ceremony.

Only when it was too late did my mother realise that

her sons, each chained to his keyboard as a performer, would not appear for more than a moment at their sister's side. They played, I remember, like angel musicians, making the village mass, and the bare church which lacked even a belfry, radiant with music. I swaggered about, very proud of my eleven years, my long locks that made me look like a little Eve, and my pink dress, highly delighted with everything except when I looked at my sister. Very small and pale, weighed down with white silk and tulle and trembling with nervous weakness, she was gazing up at that unknown man with a swooning look of such submission on her strange, Mongolian face that the sight filled me with shame.

The violins for dancing put an end to the long meal, and at the mere sound of them the two boys quivered like wild horses. The younger, slightly tipsy, stayed where he was. But the elder, unable to bear any more, disappeared. Jumping over the wall of the Rue des Vignes, he got into our garden, wandered round the closed house, broke a window-pane and went to bed, where my mother found him when she returned, sad and weary, after handing her bewildered and trembling daughter over to the care of a man.

Long afterwards she described to me that dust-grey, early dawn of summer, her empty house that felt as though it had been pillaged, her joyless fatigue, her dress with its beaded front, and the uneasy cats summoned home by her voice and the night. She told me how she had found her elder boy asleep, his arms folded on his breast, and how his fresh mouth and closed eyes, his whole body was eloquent of that sternness of his, the sternness of the pure savage.

"Just think of it, it was so that he could be alone, far from those sweating people, and sleep caressed by the night wind, that he broke the window-pane. Was there ever a child so wise?"

I have seen him, that wise one, vault through a window on a hundred occasions, as though by a reflex action, every time there was a ring at the bell which he did not expect. When he was growing grey and prematurely aged by overwork, he could still recover the elasticity of his youth in order to leap into the garden, and his little girls would laugh to see him. Gradually his fits of misanthropy, although he struggled against them, turned his face haggard. Captive as he was, did he perhaps find his prison yard daily more confined, and remember those escapes which once upon a time used to lead him to a childish bed where he slept half-naked, chaste and voluptuously alone?

JUDITH THURMAN'S 1999 biography of Colette, *Secrets of the Flesh: A Life of Colette*, was a finalist for the National Book Award and winner of the Los Angeles Times Book Award for Biography. It has been translated into eleven languages. Her 1982 biography of Isak Dinesen, *Isak Dinesen: The Life of a Storyteller*, won the National Book Award and was the basis for Sydney Pollack's Academy Award–winning film *Out of Africa*. Ms. Thurman, a staff writer for *The New Yorker* and a contributing writer to *Architectural Digest*, lives in New York City.